SENSE OF GRACE

RICHARD F. MCGONEGAL

SENSE OF GRACE

RICHARD F. MCGONEGAL

A Cave Hollow Press Book

Warrensburg, Missouri 2020

Cave Hollow Press™

Cave Hollow Press

304 Grover Street

Warrensburg, MO 64093

Copyright 2020 by Richard F. McGonegal

Formatting and cover design by Stephanie Flint

Cover Stock Images from DepositPhotos

Library of Congress Control Number: 2019956123

Paperback Edition ISBN-13: 978-1-7342678-0-8

Cave Hollow Press™

This novel is dedicated

to my wife Kristie for her generosity of spirit,

to my daughters Heather and Jane

for their inspiration,

and to my sister Carol

for her example.

CHAPTER

1

Sheriff Francis Hood hated having blood on his hands. Hated it.

He sat on the gravel shoulder of Old Cedar Creek Road, cradling the old man's head in his lap and feeling the viscous fluid seep between his fingers and soak the right trouser leg of his uniform.

Hood didn't know who he was holding.

In the full dark of the early October morning, the light bar atop his department cruiser created strobe-like red and blue flashes revealing gray, matted hair, a stubble of beard, and a missing left ear.

The sheriff hadn't taken time to search for a wallet. As soon as he saw the blood, he called 9-1-1, sat on the roadside, lifted the man's head and applied pressure in a vain attempt to stanch the bleeding from the head wound. The man was unresponsive, but Hood knew he wasn't dead. He probably had passed out, either from shock or intoxication or both. His shallow breaths reeked with the acrid odor of stale beer and fresher vomit.

Where, Hood wondered, was the ambulance? He was tempted to look at his watch but knew it was important to maintain pressure on the wound.

The time since he called 9-1-1 seemed interminable, but he reminded himself only minutes had elapsed. Still, the persistent blood flow fueled a sense of urgency.

Hood knew better than to second-guess his decision to respond to the scene. Although he was not on duty when he heard the call on his home scanner sometime around 3:30 a.m., he answered without hesitation. He had been pacing in his kitchen, unable to sleep. Again.

When the night shift dispatcher's voice spoke from the scanner, Hood heard a welcome invitation to investigate a passing motorist's report of what appeared to be a body lying on the side of Old Cedar Creek Road. Answering the call was a chance to escape the misery and monotony of another sleepless night.

Sixty-seven days ago, his wife had taken their 14-year-old daughter Elizabeth and moved out.

He wasn't proud of counting the days. He saw it as a sign of weakness, not of strength. But it was true.

Two days after they left, he stopped drinking. He tried not to dwell on counting those days, either. He did, however, purposely memorize the date, July 28, if only because some of the folks in his recovery group said if you don't remember your sobriety date, you may not have had it yet.

Relapse was a frightening prospect for him. The past two months had been hard; he didn't want to go through that again.

Matthew, his sponsor in recovery, had assured him that if he stuck with a program his life would get better.

2

SENSE OF GRACE

So far, life had become anything but better. Since the separation, he was edgy when awake and largely unable to sleep. He would switch positions, pulling covers on and off, until finally abandoning the bed and prowling around the kitchen. That's when the obsession to drink raged in his head. He knew the alcohol would provide relief, but also knew he had to resist.

On rare occasions, like early this morning, a call on the scanner provided some respite. But, mostly, he paced, as if it would ease his cravings.

He wondered—worried, actually—about whether he would be able to stay sober. And he was haunted by numerous questions about the breakup of his family. Why did it have to come to this? Why hadn't he seen it coming? What could he do to fix it?

He had no answers.

Neither did Matthew. Instead, Matthew advised patience and offered recovery-program platitudes: "Life on life's terms," "This, too, will pass," "Easy does it."

Hood was sick of hearing them. He considered himself a problem solver.

He looked down at the man whose head was in his lap, at the blood that continued to seep between his fingers.

"Some problem solver," he silently chided himself. "This guy could bleed out right here in my lap." His frustration and impatience multiplied with each passing moment until he heard, finally, the distant sound of an approaching siren.

* * * * *

Hood used his key card to unlock the solid oak door with the words Huhman County Sheriff's Department emblazoned in black block letters shadowed in gold.

The department occupied half of the basement of the stately limestone courthouse serving the Central Missouri county bordered on the north by the Missouri River.

He entered and bee-lined to the double-burner coffee maker, located in an alcove near the dispatcher's station. As he fumbled to remove a disposable cup, he wondered if his eyes were as red as the coffee machine's indicator lights, which signaled almost constant use during the round-the-clock duty shifts. He scanned the mostly unoccupied desks arranged in the spacious interior, an open floor plan with the exception of two private offices—one for him and another for his chief deputy.

"You're up early," said Maggie O'Brien, the day-shift dispatcher. At age 61, Maggie was the department's senior employee and, during her nearly 40-year tenure, had witnessed Hood's ascendency from rookie deputy to sheriff.

Hood looked at the wall clock, which read 6:52 a.m. "Been up most of the night," he said. "Responded to a call early this morning."

Maggie looked at his uniform trousers. "Is that blood?"

He followed her gaze to the stain, which was nearly dry. "Yes, but it's not mine. It belongs to a guy I found on the side of the road."

"He alive?"

"Yeah," Hood answered. "Had an ear cut off."

Maggie pinched her face into a wince. "An ear?"

"Yeah. That's where I've been for the last couple hours. ER doc sent the paramedics back to look for it. I went with them."

"Find it?"

"No." Hood paused. "Damnedest thing," he added, as if to himself.

"Why don't you go home, get cleaned up, maybe take a nap."

"I will. I mean, I am. I've got a spare uniform in my office so I'm just gonna change and jot down some notes for my report while it's still fresh in my mind," he said, hoping to allay Maggie's concerns. He sensed his moodiness and erratic behavior during the last two months had triggered Maggie's maternal instincts—honed as a mother of four children and a gaggle of grandchildren. "Anything else happen overnight?"

"Break-in at A-1 Machine Company. The owner's working on a list of what was taken. A cash box was snatched from the Trivia Night fundraiser at Holy Family Catholic Church. Oh, and Young John had a fender-bender with his cruiser. He's fine." The rookie deputy had earned his nickname, Young John, not because he was young—although he was—but to differentiate him from a veteran deputy also named John. "Reports are on your desk."

"Thanks," Hood said. "Wally here?" he asked, referring to his chief deputy, Gus "Wally" Wallendorf.

"In his office."

Hood zigzagged among the desks and stopped at the open doorway of Wally's office.

A caricaturist would relish the stark contrasts presented by the two men. Hood was a study of muscle and curved lines. He stood nearly six feet and weighed about 210 pounds. His biceps, forearms, thighs, and calves were thick, his shoulders and chest broad, and his waist trim. His round head was topped with short, sandy-brown hair and his face was dominated by a natural, almost perpetual, smile.

Wally, however, was all angles and sharp lines. He was lanky, sinewy, and six feet, four inches tall. His face was lean, almost gaunt, with narrow eyes, thin lips, and a tangle of unruly brown hair. Wally's uniform seemed to dangle from his skeletal body, whereas Hood's uniform was well-fitted and, typically, worn with military precision.

Today was an exception. As he stood in Wally's doorway, Hood's wrinkled shirt was partially untucked, his shoes were scuffed and muddy, and the stained trouser leg demanded attention.

Wally immediately focused on the stain. "You okay?" he asked.

"Fine," Hood said. He waved a hand dismissively. "Guy got his ear cut off. Spent the last hour or so looking for it."

"Wanna tell me about it?"

"Sure," Hood said. He stepped into the office, sat, and related the story.

When he was finished, Wally asked, "This guy have a name?"

"Yeah, I wrote it down." At the ER, Hood had looked through the man's wallet and found identification for the hospital's admission form and for his own report. "I swear I've heard the name before, but I can't place it," he added, as he removed a notebook from his shirt pocket and began flipping pages. "Ah, here it is—Jacob Grace."

"Jacob Grace," Wally repeated.

"Ring a bell?"

"Hell, yeah. If it's the same Jacob Grace, it's the guy who massacred his family way back when."

The connection caused Hood to cringe.

"We got a Department of Corrections notice a few weeks ago about his pending release." Wally rummaged through a stack of papers, retrieved a document and passed it to his boss. "This the guy?"

The familiar face of Jacob Grace, with both ears, stared at Hood as he looked at the memo. He recalled little about the killings, which had occurred nearly thirty years ago. At the time, he was a high school student who was more interested in Cheryl Verslues, his Chevelle SS, and hunting and fishing, not necessarily in that order. "You remember anything about those murders?" he asked Wally.

"I was, like, nine," Wally said. "Ask Maggie. I heard her talking about it the day we got the notice from Corrections. She seemed to remember quite a bit."

"Ask if she can come in here for a few minutes," Hood said. "I need to call the hospital real quick."

While Wally conversed with Maggie, Hood used his cell

phone to contact the ER supervisor and inform her of Jacob's criminal history so she could determine what security precautions, if any, were needed. He also said he wanted to question Jacob before he was discharged and was assured the patient wouldn't be released before noon. Satisfied, he disconnected.

Moments later, Maggie joined them and listened while Hood briefed her on the identity of the man with the missing ear.

"Jacob Grace," Maggie said. "Oh my."

Hood knew from experience that few revelations merited an "Oh my" from Maggie. "So," he asked. "What can you tell us?"

"Well," she said, "that was just short of thirty years ago; the anniversary should be coming up later this month. I remember because it was the first major case we were involved in after I was promoted to dispatcher. As you can imagine, it shook up not just the law enforcement folks, but the whole community—even made national headlines."

She inhaled a long breath and folded her hands in her lap. "Jacob was arrested for killing his wife and the two boys. They were just children. And he used a knife, a big kitchen knife. I remember Sheriff Westerman and the deputies who worked the scene walked around here like zombies for a while. They were traumatized."

Hood tried, but failed, to conjure a zombie-like image of his long-time predecessor, Cliff Westerman.

"I saw the photos," Maggie continued. "Blood was

everywhere—on the furniture, floors, walls."

Hood knew from the tremor in her hands that her recollection was creating an all-too-vivid picture.

"They were all slashed and stabbed to death," she added. "All except one—little Angela. She was maybe seven or eight at the time. She was cut badly, especially her face, but she survived."

Maggie looked up at her boss, and Hood waited for her pained expression to diminish as the images faded.

"Do we still have the files?"

"They're paper, not electronic. I helped store the older files in the annex some years ago. I'm pretty sure they're still there. I'll check."

Hood was eager to learn more but reluctant to drag Maggie back into the raw recesses of memory. She had provided some background; now it was his job to learn more from the files and from Jacob Grace himself. Still, he had one more question for Maggie.

"This Angela Grace, the daughter, is she the—?"

"The artist and illustrator," Maggie said. "She's made quite a name for herself. She could probably live anywhere—New York, Los Angeles. Why she chooses to stay in that old farmhouse where it all happened is a mystery to me."

CHAPTER

2

The Grace family farmhouse looked better than Hood remembered.

When he was a child—sitting with his older sister in the back seat of his dad's 1978 Chevrolet Impala station wagon—his family passed the Grace house each Sunday on the way to church.

Hood turned into the long gravel driveway and parked beside an immaculate Cadillac SUV. The once shabby house was similarly pristine. The white clapboard was either freshly painted or power washed, the colonial blue shutters and porch accents gleamed, and the shrubs were pruned to enhance their natural growth, not coerced into artificial, geometric shapes.

Like Maggie, Hood was puzzled. Maggie's words—"Why she chooses to stay in the old farmhouse where it all happened is a mystery to me"—echoed in his mind.

Hood was eager to talk with Angela Grace. If she knew nothing about the attack, he felt obligated to inform her before she learned it from another source, particularly social media. But he also wanted to gauge her reaction. He knew, both from training and experience, that family members were among the prime suspects in violent crimes. Without jumping to conclusions, he had to consider the sole survivor of a family massacre had one hell of a motive to commit an act of vengeance.

He climbed the porch and knocked on the door.

The woman who opened it was younger than he had expected. She was squat and round, as if some fairy tale giant had pressed his thumb on the top of her head and squashed her facial features and stature. She wore a shapeless black top and baggy black pants. Her skin was slack and doughy, with colorful tattoos completely or partially visible on her neck, wrists, and ankles.

"Ms. Grace. I'm your sheriff, Francis Hood."

The woman scrutinized him. "I'm not Angela Grace," she corrected. "I'm Odessa."

"Sorry," Hood said. "Is Ms. Grace available?"

"Not without an appointment. I can take your name—"

"This is official business," Hood said, switching his tone from courteous to officious.

"Nevertheless, Miss Grace, Angela, does not see people without an appointment."

Hood paused, inhaled a long breath. "Look—Odessa is it? I have information I must discuss."

"It's okay, Odessa," a voice interrupted. "I'll see him in the parlor. Let me know when it's time." Hood looked beyond Odessa into a long, darkened hallway, but saw no one.

"Very well," Odessa said, her reluctance apparent.

"Follow me."

The interior Hood entered was dim, with the exception of an open doorway at the end of the long corridor that opened to a windowed room illuminated by bright sunlight.

Odessa, however, did not lead him to that room. Instead, she motioned him to the right, into a large, darkened parlor illuminated only by a table lamp and shafts of sunlight penetrating between heavy, funereal draperies.

"Please, have a seat," Odessa said, as much a demand as an invitation. She motioned Hood to one of two vintage armchairs covered in flocked fabric. He scanned the room, which struck him as a throwback to earlier times. In addition to the armchairs, the furnishings—aged, if not antique—included a sofa that matched the armchairs, a baby grand piano, a roll top desk, and two barrister bookcases displaying an array of hardbound books.

Hood sat.

"Now," she said. "Please remain seated. Don't rise when Angela enters, and under no circumstances are you to approach her or touch her. Prince won't like it."

Hood's expression betrayed his confusion, but he said nothing.

"In addition, use your normal speaking voice, but avoid making any rhythmic noises. No humming, whistling, toe tapping—that sort or thing. Understood?"

Hood nodded.

"I need you to tell me you understand."

"I understand."

"Good. Angela will be with you momentarily," Odessa

concluded, then left the room.

While he waited, Hood considered the instructions. He had encountered a fair share of quirky situations, and this one had potential to rank high on the list.

He tried to picture Angela Grace—her appearance, her demeanor—but he was not prepared for the woman who entered.

The first thing he noticed was the veil that covered her face below the eyes. He wondered if she wore it intentionally to send some message, or to disguise visible scars or some flaw of facial reconstruction. He found himself trying to imagine how the obscured nose, mouth, cheeks, and chin matched her wide, lustrous silver-blue eyes and the long, straight daffodil blonde hair that seemed almost to glow in the darkened room. She moved like a dancer, her lithe but shapely figure accentuated by a navy blue turtleneck sweater and fitted jeans.

Hood realized he was staring and instinctively started to rise as she approached, but reconsidered when he saw her companion, a beautifully marked, muscular German Shepherd that trotted beside her and eyed him warily.

Angela sat on the sofa facing Hood, but the dog stood at attention. Hood had been around enough attack-trained dogs to recognize one.

"I'm Angela Grace," she said.

"I'm your sheriff, Francis Hood."

"And this," she said, nodding at the dog, "is Prince. He likes to check out strangers. Do you mind?"

"Not at all." Hood liked dogs. He fondly recalled his younger years hiking and hunting with his father, accompanied by the pack of beagles his father raised.

Angela whispered a command in what Hood guessed was German, and Prince approached. He cautiously held out his hand, which Prince sniffed before leaning into the sheriff's knee and accepting gentle pats on his flank.

At a follow-up command, Prince returned to his owner and sat at her feet, but remained alert. "So," Angela asked. "How may I help you?"

"You're the daughter of Jacob Grace? Is that correct?"

"Yes."

"Were you advised that your father has been released from the custody of the Department of Corrections?"

"Yes. I received notice of a victims' impact panel hearing about two months ago and another letter about three weeks ago advising me his release date would be October 1. So, I'm guessing he's been out three days now."

"Yes, well, he was assaulted last night. I found him on the side of the road early this morning and went with him to the hospital."

Although Hood had tried to anticipate any reactions or questions she would have, he was surprised when she stood, prompting Prince to follow her lead. "If that's what you've come to tell me, Sheriff, thank you for doing your duty. I'll have Odessa see you out."

Hood remained seated. "Someone cut his ear off," he said, intentionally trying to elicit further reaction.

Instead, she repeated, "Thank you, Sheriff, Odessa will see you out."

"Do you know of anyone who might—"

"Sheriff," she interrupted. "I don't mean to be rude. I know you have a job to do, and you seem very earnest, but I have no idea who assaulted my father, nor do I care."

Hood, who preferred speaking with people at eye level, arose from his chair, immediately drawing Prince's attention. "Have you had any contact with your father since his release?"

"None."

"Look I don't mean—" Hood lifted his hands in a gesture of apology.

Angela flinched ever so slightly, and the dog tensed, prompting her to whisper a reassuring word, again in German.

"I'm sorry to dredge up old memories," he continued, careful to remain still, "but—"

"They're not old memories," she said. "I'm reminded every morning when I wake up and look in the mirror. I live with them every day."

"I'm just—" Hood began, his frustration apparent. "I'm just trying to find out who assaulted your father."

"Very well. Then let me assure you I have nothing to offer. I haven't seen my father in nearly thirty years, and I intend to keep it that way."

As she spoke, Odessa appeared in the doorway. Both Hood and Angela looked at her.

"Ethan's on the phone," Odessa said to Angela. "Says it's urgent."

"With Ethan, everything's urgent," Angela said, with a hint of sarcasm not lost on Hood. She turned to the sheriff. "I need to take this," she added. "Please, excuse me. Odessa—"

"Will see me out," Hood said, completing her remark. "Yes, I know."

CHAPTER

3

Back at the hospital ER, Hood approached the nurses' station, introduced himself to a nurse named Rachel—according to her photo ID—and inquired about Jacob Grace.

"Let me just check with Dr. Daniels," she said. "He just finished his examination—"

"Steve Daniels?" Hood asked.

"Stephen, yes."

"Is he here?"

"Yes, he's just back there dictating his notes."

Hood looked over Rachel's shoulder to a glass-enclosed rectangular area where the back of Dr. Daniels' broad shoulders and balding, square-shaped head were visible. Hood considered the presence of the ear, nose, and throat specialist as an encouraging sign in what, so far, had been an unproductive morning.

"Tell him Sheriff Francis Hood would like to see him."

"Very well."

He watched as Rachel walked to the enclosure and relayed his request, prompting Daniels to turn and wave for

Hood to join him.

Hood guessed—based on the doctor's thinning, grey hair—that he was nearing retirement age. Daniels' deep-set eyes and haunted look seemed rooted in a deep malaise. The sheriff didn't know the doctor well, but the two had become acquainted while serving on the local Salvation Army board and as committee chairmen for a recent United Way fundraising campaign. Hood considered these volunteer positions to be perfunctory duties expected of so-called community leaders.

The sheriff entered the glass enclosure, and the two men greeted each other with a handshake and shared a brief conversation about prospects for the upcoming fundraiser.

"So," Daniels said, "what can I do for you?"

"What can you tell me about Jacob Grace?"

"Well, between doctor-patient confidentiality and federal privacy rules, not a lot. Besides, the ER staff did most of the work. I was here making rounds and was asked to take a look at him."

"He's not a regular patient?"

"No," Daniels said. "He doesn't have a physician, so I may just have inherited him, by default."

"Do you know who he is? His background, I mean?"

"One of the nurses briefed me. Said you called to alert the staff."

"I wanted to give you guys a heads-up in case you wanted your security people on stand-by."

"As far as I know, he hasn't been any problem, but then, he's coming off one hell of a bender."

Hood chuffed. "Knew that as soon as his first breath hit me."

"ER doc was worried about alcohol poisoning, so he ordered a BAC."

BAC, Hood knew, was the acronym for blood-alcohol content. "Any results yet?"

Daniels paged back in the report. "Here it is," he said. "He posted a 2.6."

The number was not only more than three times the legal limit to drive, but it indicated severe impairment. "That's high." Hood mused aloud. "Maybe he passed out before he was attacked. I didn't see much sign of a struggle."

Daniels nodded agreement. "There were superficial cuts on his head and neck indicating he thrashed around, and scuffs and bruises on his knees and elbows, but the real damage was the missing ear."

"Any idea what was used to cut it off?"

"It was a clean cut, so I'm guessing a very sharp blade— a razor, maybe."

"Could the ear be reattached?"

"I was told it wasn't found."

"That's why I'm asking. I keep wondering why his attacker would take the ear. Obviously, Jacob didn't do it himself, or we would have found the ear, the weapon, or some trail of blood."

Daniels shrugged. "Don't know."

"Me neither. Maybe the assailant kept it as a trophy. That way it couldn't be reattached."

"There's always prosthetics," Daniels said. "You'd be

amazed—"

"But they're expensive, right? I'm thinking Jacob Grace is in no position to afford a prosthetic ear."

Again, Daniels shrugged.

"Is he awake?"

"He was when I left him. I just sent a nurse to his room to give him follow-up instructions"

"Sober?"

"Should be by now. Probably hung over," the doctor replied. "He didn't have much to say. At least not to me."

"I think it's time I had a talk with him. Care to join me?"

"Normally I'd say no, but you've got my curiosity up."

They walked to the room, knocked, and entered. Jacob, who was seated in a chair, started to rise, but stopped; obviously expecting to be discharged, not delayed, he grimaced and dropped back into the chair. Rachel stood beside him, holding a pen poised above a clipboard.

Hood thought the patient looked pathetic—silly, even. A bandage wrapped around his head covered the ear hole, but not the area where his head and left cheek had been shaved. Elsewhere, his thin, greying hair protruded without direction, and stubble peppered his chin and neck.

"Oh," Rachel said, obviously surprised by the appearance of the sheriff and doctor. "I made the appointment for Mr. Grace to see you in your office next week."

"And I was about to say I got no money," Jacob said.

"Medicare?" Rachel asked.

"Yeah," Jacob answered. "Signed me up for that in prison."

SENSE OF GRACE

Rachel looked to the doctor, who nodded approval. "I guess that's it then."

She left the room. Daniels remained standing near the door while Hood approached the patient.

"I'm your sheriff, Francis Hood."

Jacob said nothing.

"I'm the one who found you on the side of the road this morning."

Hood expected at least a nod of acknowledgement but detected none. "What can you tell me about last night?" he continued.

Jacob looked from Hood to Daniels. "Can I go?" he asked the doctor.

"I think the sheriff wants to ask you a few questions," Daniels answered.

Jacob looked back at Hood, who repeated his question.

"I don't remember," Jacob said.

Hood was uncertain whether the man was being difficult or truthful. From his own experience with blackouts, he was acutely aware of the inability to recall what had happened the previous evening—whether it was the final score of a Cardinals game or even what he had for dinner.

"I smelled alcohol on your breath," Hood said. "Were you drinking?"

"Had a few beers at The Hideaway."

Hood was familiar with The Hideaway, a popular roadhouse on Old Cedar Creek Road, less than a mile from where he had found Jacob.

"I was walking back to where I'm staying," Jacob added. He paused. Confusion clouded his expression. "That's all I remember."

"Do you remember being attacked?"

Jacob hesitated, as if searching for the memory. "No."

"Know of anyone who might have a reason to attack you, cut off your ear?"

Again, Jacob hesitated, then asked, "You know who I am?"

"You're Jacob Grace," Hood answered.

"You know what I done?"

Hood nodded.

"There's your answer," Jacob said.

Hood frowned. Jacob's answers weren't helping narrow the range of suspects. "You said you were walking to where you're staying. Where's that?"

"Staying with Hutch."

"Jesse Hutchschreider?" Hood knew Hutch, an ex-con who preached at a small, rural Huhman County church. Hutch ran a modest cattle operation and boarded horses.

"Yeah. He's letting me stay in his stable if I help with stuff." He paused briefly. "Can I go now?"

Hood turned to Daniels. "I'm done," he said, frustration evident in his tone.

Hood was delightfully surprised to find his wife's van parked outside the family home.

He parked in the driveway, got out of his cruiser, and

rubbed the stubble on his chin. His intention was to shave, shower, and perhaps nap—if he could sleep—before returning to the office.

"Hello," he called as he entered the front door, directing his voice up the stairs, where he expected Linda to be.

"In the kitchen," she answered.

The sound of her voice cheered him. Although they had been separated more than two months—which roughly coincided with his time in recovery—they communicated as they worked toward what Hood hoped would be reconciliation. In the meantime, Linda and their daughter, 14-year-old Elizabeth, were staying at the home of Otto and Sarah Kampeter. Sarah was Linda's younger sister, and Otto was her husband.

Hood entered the kitchen and saw Linda rummaging through the drawer where larger utensils—spatulas, whisks, serving spoons—were kept.

"Hi," Hood said. "I didn't expect to find you here."

"I came for my mixer," she said. "Sarah doesn't have one, and I'm making a cake for the church bake sale tonight. Can't seem to find the beaters, though."

"Well, I haven't used them," he quipped.

She looked up and smiled. "What are you doing home?"

"Long story. Responded to an assault. Guy got his ear cut off. Thought I'd get cleaned up."

She resumed rummaging.

"How's Elizabeth?" Hood asked.

"Typical freshman. Thinks she knows everything and doesn't need any advice from Mom. Except when it comes to boys. Then she's clueless."

Hood smiled in an effort to mask any hint of self-pity. He missed spending time with his wife and daughter and hoped the separation would end soon.

He and Linda had met while attending Huhman County R-1 High School and dated casually as seniors. After graduation, they literally went in opposite directions; he traveled west and earned a bachelor's in criminal justice from University of Missouri-Kansas City; she headed east to Maryville University in St. Louis, where she received her nursing degree. The attraction of job opportunities and families eventually brought them back to Huhman County, where a chance encounter led them to resume dating and, in time, to the altar.

Hood was happy in his marriage. At age 46, they recently had celebrated their twenty-second anniversary, and he hadn't yet experienced anything he would describe as a mid-life crisis. Although he never considered their relationship one that burned with a white-hot flame, it was warm and comfortable.

"So," Linda asked, interrupting his musings, "how's everything with you?"

"Good," he answered. "Still sober. It's getting—I don't know if easier is the right word—but better. I still have cravings, but they're not as bad, and they don't seem to come as often. I'm learning some ways to get through it."

"I'm proud of you."

Hood knew she meant it. She didn't lack sincerity or fear showing it. "The group's a big help. And Matthew," he added, referring to his sponsor.

"Sarah tells me she still thinks about drinking sometimes, and she's been in recovery for a while now."

"How are Sarah and Otto?"

"They're good. I think I consider Elizabeth and me more of a burden to them than they do. They're so gracious, so giving. I'm thankful for them every day."

Hood nodded but said nothing. He had, on numerous occasions during the past two months, encouraged her to come home. Each time, she declined, saying the time wasn't right. Hood knew she didn't want, perhaps couldn't endure, having her hopes shattered again. He reminded himself of one of the program's slogans—"one day at a time." He knew his pleading would be seen as another attempt to manipulate and control the situation. He knew his words were hollow; action, continued sobriety, was necessary. Even then, there were no guarantees.

"Can I take you and Elizabeth out to dinner tomorrow night?" he asked, breaking the awkward silence.

"That would be nice."

CHAPTER

4

Hood showered and attempted to nap, but thoughts of Angela, Jacob, Linda, and Elizabeth intruded, as did the words of his recovery sponsor, Matthew.

"Don't overcomplicate it," Matthew had counseled once he discovered the sheriff took an analytical approach to problem solving. "Keep it simple."

Hood tried, but his mind raced. He felt some anxiety about dinner with his wife and daughter. He knew the feeling was silly, but uneasiness lingered—like being unprepared for an upcoming interview.

He intentionally turned his thoughts to the assault and replayed the events of the morning.

Because Angela was the lone survivor of Jacob's rampage, she had to be considered the prime suspect in the attack on her father. Although Hood thought she seemed genuinely surprised by the news, he conceded her veil hid much of her reaction. He wondered if it was a regular accessory or if she wore it specifically for their meeting. But he also had to consider the possibility she was not responsible, which left—as Jacob had remarked at the hospital—anyone else familiar with, connected to, or affected by the massacre.

Clues were scarce. The Hideaway, where Jacob had been drinking prior to the assault, seemed as good a starting point as any.

Hood put on a clean uniform and retraced his drive to Old Cedar Creek Road. As he steered into The Hideaway's gravel parking area, he noticed "Mama" Luella Mengwasser's Ford Econoline van—faded white with rusted wheel wells and a missing hub cap—parked in a far corner. He knew the restaurant wasn't open yet, but the presence of the van indicated Mama was on the job.

Mama's home cooking had been the main attraction for years at the St. Peter's Fall Festival, so much so that she and her husband were encouraged to open a family restaurant. They did, and all went well until her husband's death, when the establishment gradually became more bar than grill and the reputation morphed into its being a roadhouse for roughnecks.

But Mama, a self-described "tough cookie," somehow managed to convince a core group of young toughs to practice a zero-tolerance policy regarding fighting, arguing, or harassing the paying customers. Known collectively as "Mama's boys," they accepted her challenge to keep peace. As a result, The Hideaway began to attract a diverse clientele—bikers, professionals, barflies, farmers, families— all united in the expectation of fabulous food and a hassle-free atmosphere.

Hood parked his cruiser, got out, and rapped on the door.

"Closed," Mama's raspy voice shouted from within.

"It's your sheriff, Francis Hood."

"Hang on, Francis," she hollered.

Moments later, he heard the deadbolt turn from within.

"Hey, Francis," Mama greeted when she opened the door. "To what do I owe the pleasure?"

"Need to ask you a few questions."

"C'mon in. You don't mind me unpackin' some stock while we talk, do ya?"

"Not at all." Hood entered, pausing to allow his pupils to adjust to the dimness, which reminded him of Angela Grace's parlor.

"Savin' 'lectricity," Mama said as she flicked a series of switches and illuminated the expansive dining room, which was large enough to accommodate an array of round tables surrounded by chairs, a row of booths and, opposite, a long bar, a pool table, and several pinball and electronic game machines.

While Mama went behind the bar and began transferring liquor bottles from a cardboard carton onto mirrored shelves, Hood perched on a stool and asked, "Were you here last night?"

"Last night, the night before that, and however many before that. You'd think the owner would give herself a night off once in a while."

"You know most of your customers, right?"

"You bet."

"You know Jacob Grace?"

Mama stopped, as if immobilized, holding a bottle in each hand. "I'll be damned," she said. "I thought I knew that old coot from somewhere." She paused. "I'll be. That was Jacob?"

"He said he was here last night."

"Had to be him," she said, although she shook her head in disbelief. "He sat in that booth right over there."

"By himself?"

"Yep."

"Did he talk to anyone?"

"Nope. Just sat there and got drunk 'til he leaned over and puked on the floor. I threw his ass out."

"When was that?"

"Around midnight."

"Did you notice anybody watching him? Anyone follow him out or leave right after he did?"

"Not that I noticed."

"None of Mama's Boys went out to teach him a lesson about puking on your floor?"

"Not that I saw." She positioned a bottle on the shelf. "What's this all about, Francis?"

"Someone assaulted Jacob Grace and left him lying on the side of the road about a half mile from here."

"After what he did to his family, ain't surprised somebody beat 'im up."

"He got more than a beating; he got his ear cut off."

Mama stared at him. "Rough justice," she said.

Later in the day, while Hood changed from his uniform into casual clothes, two other men sat in the front seat of a

1991 Olds Cutlass and watched the front of St. Michael's Catholic Church and its adjoining annex/gymnasium.

"Easy money," said Randy Knaebel. He sat behind the wheel of the car, which continued to run reliably despite its battered body, chipped navy blue paint, and rusted rear bumper.

"I dunno, man," said J.T. Johnson, who sat in the torn passenger seat. "Doin' a church just seems like bad"—he fumbled for the word—"you know." In his native St. Louis, J.T. was known by his street name, "Jet."

"It's a simple grab and go," Randy said, referring to the plan they had worked out. "Besides, we ain't goin' in the church. This is just another money-maker they have in the gym." He gnawed on a wooden toothpick as he leaned out the open side window and surveyed the site of the annual St. Michael's Sodality Sale-A-Rama.

Randy, a Huhman County native, remembered attending the long-running event with his mother when he was a boy. He remembered entering a massive doorway and climbing a short stairwell to a landing where his mother would purchase tickets from a pair of elderly ladies seated at a folding table. Randy would stare at the stacks of bills in the metal cash box before his mother ushered him through a double doorway that opened to reveal aisles and aisles of "treasure": arts and crafts, brownies and cakes, quilts, and sparkling holiday ornaments.

The Sale-A-Rama had marked Randy's debut as a thief. Using his "good" hand—not his deformed, claw-like right—he would pocket a cupcake to be eaten later or pilfer a potholder he could trade with one of the smart girls for answers to a homework assignment.

He was uprooted from Huhman County at age eight, when his mother divorced Randy's father. The dissolution included restoration of her maiden name, Knaebel, to distinguish her, she said, from that "philandering louse."

Together, mother and son relocated to Florida, the first stop in a series of nomadic moves. A constant throughout their travels was Randy's delinquent behavior, including alcohol and illegal drug use, breaking and entering, and stealing.

The last stop before Randy's recent return to Huhman County was in St. Louis, where his mother was diagnosed with terminal cancer. During that period, Randy got to know Jet, a young black man who lived in the same apartment complex.

Their casual acquaintance took on another dimension one evening when Jet interceded on Randy's behalf after Randy was stopped on the street by three members of a gang wearing jackets identifying them as Street Kings. Although Jet was only a fledgling member, his older brother was a respected King who died shielding one of his peers during a drive-by shooting. Jet defused the threat, and Randy walked away unscathed.

Less than two months later, Randy was able to return the favor.

The Street Kings had put Jet to the test by including him in a major drug deal, which ended with one member dead, another wounded, no money and no drugs. Jet, who was blamed for the botched exchange, needed to make himself scarce—immediately.

At the time, Randy was considering a return to Huhman County. His mother had died, and he never had felt at home in the dingy, soulless city. When he learned of Jet's plight, he offered to bring Jet with him to the relative obscurity of Central Missouri. Jet accepted without hesitation.

Randy chewed the toothpick and shifted his gaze from the St. Michael's annex to Jet. "You ready?"

"Been wondering what the fuck we're waiting for."

"Okay, let's do it."

They exited the Cutlass and crossed the street. Randy spit the toothpick onto the sidewalk and peeked into the small rectangular glass in the front door. The scene was similar to what he remembered; two elderly people—tonight a man and a woman—sat at a folding table on a landing a short staircase away.

Both men pulled ski masks over their faces. Jet put on gloves; Randy used his teeth to pull on one glove and one mitten, then hid his mittened right in a jacket pocket. They nodded to each other, opened the door, and bounded up the stairs.

"Nobody scream," Randy warned, pointing at them through his jacket pocket.

The thin, white-haired woman, who looked nearly lifeless, screamed like a banshee on fire. Her unexpected shriek terrified Randy in the same moment he realized it was not part of the plan, and he would have to improvise. "Shut up," he demanded, then turned to Jet, who slapped the old woman, slammed the lid on the cash box, and snatched it from the table.

"Go, go, go," Randy yelled—as if he somehow had regained control of the situation—but Jet already was heading down the stairs. As Randy followed, he heard the gymnasium doors behind him open, releasing background chatter from the Sale-A-Rama and an exchange of concerned voices.

Randy sprinted across the street, using his teeth to pull off his left glove, which he spat into the driver's seat. He fumbled the key ring momentarily while removing it from his pocket, but quickly recovered and deftly used his left hand to insert the key in the slot designed for right-handed drivers. The ignition fired just as a wave of too many people burst though the annex doorway and flowed onto the sidewalk.

"Get us the fuck outta here," Jet shrieked.

The Cutlass lurched and immediately drew attention from the crowd. Arms were raised and fingers pointed as men rushed toward them.

Randy pressed the accelerator and watched in the rear view mirror as his pursuers receded.

They were two streets away before either man spoke.

"Easy money, my ass," Jet said.

The St. Cecilia Catholic Church basement was a venue for a variety of sacred and secular activities.

The colorful array of toys and blocks, groups of tables and chairs, a hardwood floor and basketball hoops, and an adjoining kitchen revealed some of its multiple functions as nursery, classroom, gymnasium, wedding reception site, and, on occasion, voting precinct.

On Thursday evenings, it served as the gathering place for Recovery Rules, a weekly meeting hosted by Hood's sponsor Matthew.

Although Matthew included 12-step concepts, he didn't stick to them exclusively, and he deviated from the format followed by other groups. He occasionally would invite guest speakers or introduce materials from other disciplines, including organized religion, philosophy, psychology, and medicine.

All addicts were welcome. Alcoholics and drug addicts made up the majority of the regulars, but some participants shared their struggles with eating disorders or with gambling or pornography addictions.

When Hood entered, Matthew was in the kitchen making coffee, and some of the early arrivals were seated at the rectangular arrangement of tables. As Hood approached, he noticed one of the chairs—displaying a "Reserved" sign—remained folded and propped against the table.

Hood was curious about the sign. Although he had attended previous meetings when Matthew had invited a speaker, no seat had been similarly marked. Hood sat to the left of Mac, one of the venerated "old timers" in the program, then listened to the banter and small talk—the lack of rain, the failure of the Cardinals and Royals to reach the playoffs—as others gathered.

Hood hadn't met any of the regulars before joining the

group and hadn't socialized with any of them outside the meetings. What little he knew from observations and conversations before and after the meetings was that the diverse members were united by the common denominator of addiction.

The conversation diminished when Matthew approached and set carafes of coffee—one regular and one decaf—on the table. Hood was reminded of a classroom of unruly students becoming silent and attentive when their teacher entered.

"I want to welcome everyone tonight," Matthew said to the nine other participants in attendance. Normally, he seated himself before he spoke, but he remained standing. "As you may have noticed, I reserved a seat tonight." He walked to the designated chair and unfolded it. "Jean, one of our regulars, died yesterday."

A collective breath and scattered whispers were audible as Matthew moved to his customary spot and sat. "Although she won't be with us tonight—at least, not physically—she is with us in spirit. And spirituality is the topic I'd like for us to discuss tonight.

"The program of recovery suggests we connect to a power greater than ourselves, which can be very different from practicing a specific religion. Jean often shared that she didn't consider herself a religious person—she didn't belong to a denomination or attend church regularly—but she was humble, grateful, and giving, and I'm convinced she was a spiritual person. So the question I'd like to begin with tonight is: Do you consider yourself a spiritual person, and what does that mean to you?"

A brief silence ensued before the man sitting to Hood's right said, "I'm a grateful alcoholic today and my name is Greg."

Because the order of sharing routinely followed a clockwise or counter-clockwise direction around the table, Hood wondered if he would be next or last. He consciously tried to avoid that thought and focus on Greg's comments.

"Today, I'm living another day sober thanks to my Lord and Savior, Jesus Christ," Greg said. "I was a Christian before I became an alcoholic, but I drank away my job and the money we were saving for my kid's college and nearly broke up my family. I knew I had strayed from God's plan, and I knew I needed to reconnect with him, so I guess I had some kind of advantage over people who say they struggle with a higher power. Spirituality isn't a problem, but tolerance is. For me, Jesus is the truth and, therefore, anything else must be false. In recovery, at least I'm becoming more tolerant of other people's beliefs, or lack of belief." He sighed. "I'll pass," he concluded, indicating he had finished speaking.

"Thanks Greg," a chorus of voices said.

Matthew looked to Greg's left and right, seemed somehow to sense Hood's tension, and said, "Jenny?"

"Jenny, alcoholic," she said, straightening from her slouch. "I was pissed at God for the longest time. Some of you know my story. My parents were hypocrites of the first order. Mom and Dad went to church every Sunday, but Dad had evil tendencies when it came to me, and Mom covered up for him.

When I ran away, I left behind everything they represented, including church. But, you know, in recovery, I've learned there's a difference between religion and spirituality. I can't say I love God, but I'm not pissed anymore. I guess that's something. Pass."

"Thanks Jenny," came the familiar refrain.

As the sharing continued, Hood found himself listening less and thinking more about what he would say when his turn came. He had been in recovery about two months and felt he was just beginning to grasp the language, the slogans, and the concepts. Although Matthew had been helpful, Hood felt he was making slow progress in an unfamiliar process. He had attended Sunday church services intermittently with Linda and Elizabeth, but rarely devoted much thought to spirituality or other concepts he considered beyond his understanding and, certainly, beyond his ability to control.

Before he had decided what he would say, the sharing had circulated to Mac, who was introducing himself.

"Quite frankly," Mac said, "I really didn't think much about spirituality when I first got into recovery, so when people started talking about how they couldn't quit on their own and had to surrender to a higher power to stay sober, that didn't make any sense to me. I wasn't looking for a higher power. I was looking to stop drinking, to blackout or pass-out drunk every night. I was never able to quit on my own—believe me, I tried—but I listened to what people said about being open to the possibility of a higher power, and I didn't drink that day, or the next day, or the next. So it dawned on me that if I could never stay sober by myself, but I wasn't drinking, maybe something else was at work. That was my first introduction to a higher power, and the more time I spend here, the more I've experienced how that works in my life." Mac paused. "And I'm grateful for that. I pass."

The attention and anticipation of the participants shifted to Hood, who looked at the table, avoiding eye contact. "Hi, my name's Francis and I'm an alcoholic," he said. "I think I'll just listen tonight."

CHAPTER

5

Sleep eluded Hood.

Angela Grace was in his head. Her unique history, unusual choices, and veiled face teased his curiosity.

He arose from bed, went downstairs, and switched on his computer. He typed Angela Grace into a keyword search and scanned the results, which included a story from a three-year-old issue of *Artistry* magazine.

He opened it and read the title: "The Sensory World of Angela Grace," by Victoria Martin.

Beside the text was a photograph from an exhibit featuring a masked Angela in a gallery setting. He paged down to other images of a veiled or masked Angela at shows and receptions, examples of her artwork, and a posed picture of an eight-year-old Angela, captioned as her third-grade photograph, taken before the massacre.

Returning to the top of the story, Hood began reading.

Angela Grace paints not only what she sees, but what she hears. She arrived on the art scene as an illustrator of children's books, but the mystique surrounding her inclusion of hidden objects vaulted her into the realm of fine arts exhibits and galleries.

Her rise in popularity can be traced to celebrated art critic Stan Highmore's praise of Ms. Grace's unique approach to shapes and color, which she translates from songs, rhythmic patterns, and musical phrasings she hears.

Ms. Grace experiences a form of synesthesia, described as a neurological condition in which one sensory stimulation evokes an involuntary, second sensation. As a synesthete, she is among an estimated five percent of the population. More than sixty types of synesthesia have been reported, and include smelling sounds, tasting words, and hearing shapes.

The condition is not new. Experiences of synesthesia—including reports from renowned authors, artists and composers—date back centuries. Ms. Grace experiences a form of chromaesthesia; for her, tones, and notes—particularly repetitive rhythms—trigger visual images, which she captures in her art.

Odessa's admonition to avoid rhythmic sounds in Angela's presence suddenly made sense. Hood continued reading.

Although her creation of visual art linked to sound attracted attention, it was the ironic discovery of menacing images—razors, knives, and assorted sharp objects—hidden in her children's book illustrations that catapulted her career.

Suddenly, finding these troubling images in works designed for children became de rigueur in art circles—the adult equivalent of 'Where's Waldo?' searches.

Ms. Grace soon enjoyed a proliferation of commissions, and her drawings and paintings were reproduced in a commercially successful series of lithographs.

Hood scrolled to an example of her artwork and clicked on it, with the intention of enlarging the image and searching for the hidden weapon. When the image failed to enlarge, he continued reading.

A graduate of the fine arts program at Washington University in St. Louis, her original work is displayed in major galleries; reproductions decorate walls everywhere from college dorms to restaurants.

Ms. Grace's passion is a youth art school, Healing Children Through Art, which she operates in her Central Missouri hometown. She pays all the expenses for students, largely disadvantaged children.

Her connection to the art world, however, remains something of a mystery. A self-described loner, she travels only rarely to exhibit openings in major cities, including New York, Los Angeles and St. Louis. When she does appear in public, she shuns being photographed and always wears a veil or mask that reveals her eyes, but hides the remainder of her face, which was disfigured when, at age eight, she was the victim of a heinous crime.

> Angela was the sole survivor of a family massacre that took place in her childhood home, where she continues to live. Angela's mother and her two younger brothers were stabbed to death, and Angela suffered severe wounds that required extensive hospitalization. Her father, Jacob Grace, was convicted of second-degree murder and remains incarcerated at Missouri State Correctional Center.

Hood stopped reading and leaned back in his chair. Not anymore, he thought.

Maggie routinely placed the reports from overnight in Hood's in-box and centered the morning edition of the newspaper on his desk, aware that her boss began his daily office routine with updates.

When Hood settled himself behind the desk, he found a third item: a thick file folder labeled "Criminal Investigation 081887H: Grace Family Murders."

Hood picked up the newspaper, then laid it back on the desk. His thoughts—centered on the contents of the file folder—already had diverted him from his routine. He opened it, located a group of stapled pages titled "incident report," and began reading.

Narrative of Deputy Daniel Heimericks

> At 10:36 p.m. on October 13, 1988, I received a dispatch from Margaret O'Brien regarding a telephone call she

received from Mary Agnes Jobe, who lives on Route AA. Mrs. Jobe reported she and her husband Clarence heard screams coming from the neighboring Jacob Grace farm, and her husband had gone to investigate.

Deputy Ben Rackers and myself responded and arrived at the Jacob Grace residence at 10:48 p.m. Upon arrival, we observed a man, later identified as Clarence Jobe, kneeling on the front porch beside a woman, who was bleeding heavily. The man had no visible weapon and appeared to be applying pressure to an abdominal wound suffered by the victim. I instructed Deputy Rackers to call 9-1-1 for an ambulance, then exited the vehicle and drew my service weapon. As I was approaching the house, Sheriff Cliff Westerman arrived and took custody of the scene. His report follows.

Narrative of Sheriff Cliff Westerman

I arrived on the scene at 10:54 p.m. on the above date after responding to the above dispatch. I recognized Clarence Jobe as the man kneeling beside the bloodied body of Ruth Grace, wife of Jacob Grace and mother of their three children—Angela, Brian, and David.

I also drew my service weapon and, along with Deputies Heimericks and Rackers, approached the porch. In response to my questions, Clarence Jobe, who was visibly shaken, said he had arrived minutes ago, found Ruth Jobe lying on the porch, wounded and unresponsive, and had attempted to stanch the bleeding from a stomach wound.

After informing Clarence that an ambulance had been called, I performed a cursory examination and determined Ruth was not breathing and likely was dead. I directed Deputy Rackers to remain on the porch with Clarence and Ruth.

I listened for sounds from within the house but heard nothing. Deputy Heimericks and I entered through the front door, where I observed a trail of bloody footprints leading to the kitchen.

I directed Deputy Heimericks to clear the adjoining living and dining rooms while I entered the kitchen, where I observed the bloodied bodies of two children, a boy and a girl, lying on the floor. I examined them and determined both had been repeatedly stabbed and slashed, but the girl was breathing and appeared to be alive.

After Deputy Heimericks rejoined me and said the living and dining rooms were cleared, we both heard a thumping sound from the upper floor. I directed him to remain with the children, and I retraced my steps to the hall and climbed the stairs. The only sound I heard at that point was the distant sound of an approaching siren.

I cleared the master bedroom and a bathroom, then continued along the upstairs hallway, where I looked into a second bedroom, apparently a nursery. I observed a bloodied infant in a crib. The infant was not moving.

When I stepped into the room, I observed Jacob Grace seated on the floor with his back propped against a wall. His clothes were bloodstained, and in his hand he held a large kitchen knife. Jacob looked at me, his expression vacant, then plunged the blade into his stomach.

With the knife handle protruding from his abdomen, he stretched his arms and opened his mouth, but did not scream. As I rushed to him, I heard commotion from the main floor and shouted for assistance from the paramedics.

The scene became chaotic as EMTs checked each of the victims. The infant was dead. Jacob Grace was treated and readied for transport. As I returned down the stairs, I observed another EMT wheeling a stretcher carrying the girl.

Moments later, an ambulance was rushing Jacob Grace and the girl—later determined to be his daughter, Angela—to Huhman County Hospital.

The death toll included: Ruth Bunch Grace, age 33, Brian Allen Grace, age 4, and David Christopher Grace, 3 months.

Suspects

Jacob Grace is the lone suspect in the murders of his wife and two sons and the attempted murder of his daughter.

I observed him holding the knife, which is believed to be the murder weapon and currently is at the crime lab to be analyzed. In addition, I observed Jacob Grace stab himself and inflict a non-fatal wound.

Witnesses

With the exception of Jacob Grace, who has refused to cooperate or offer any statement thus far, the only partial witnesses are Clarence Jobe, a neighbor, and the sole surviving victim, daughter Angela.

Clarence Jobe said he responded to the Grace residence after he and his wife heard screams. He said he found Ruth Grace wounded and unconscious on the porch and attempted to apply pressure to an abdominal wound. He said he never entered the house and heard no sounds from within during the time before deputies arrived.

Angela Grace told a juvenile counselor from the state Division of Youth Services (see attached report by Alice LePage) she heard her parents arguing, so she took her brother Brian into the kitchen and made him a jelly sandwich. She said arguments and incidents of domestic violence are common in the household, and she and her brother typically go to another room and close the door.

On the night of the murders, she said she heard her parents arguing, followed by screams from her mother. Moments later, her father burst into the kitchen, and the look on his face was like nothing she had ever seen before. His clothes were spattered with blood, he was wielding a large knife, and he began slashing and stabbing with the knife, first at Brian and then at Angela. She tried to run but slipped and hit her head on a wooden chair. She said that's all she remembered until she awoke in the hospital. She will be interviewed further, and additional statements will be included in this file.

SENSE OF GRACE

Evidence

The bodies of the victims, their wounds, including defensive wounds, their clothing, and blood spatter at the scene are all being analyzed. Jacob Grace's clothing and the kitchen knife believed to be the murder weapon also are being analyzed.

The results will be included in this file.

Hood stopped reading and dropped the document on his desk. Although he noticed his hands were trembling, he felt numb. He reached for his coffee cup, realized it was empty, and wandered—his mind still preoccupied with the crime report—to the coffee maker, where Wally and Maggie were conversing at her dispatch station.

"St. Michael's?" he overheard Wally remark. "I'll be damned. How much did they get?"

"They're not sure," Maggie replied. "Some tickets were purchased in advance, but they think sales at the door were upwards of five hundred."

Wally watched his boss refill his cup. "You hear that, Francis?" he said. "Couple guys ripped off the Sale-A-Rama at St. Michael's."

"Haven't looked at the reports yet," Hood said. "Been reading the file on the Grace killings." He turned to Maggie, whose duties included proofreading the reports for errors and omissions before placing them on his desk. "Thanks for getting that for me, by the way."

"Sure," she said.

"Descriptions?" Hood asked.

"I'm sorry. What?" Maggie said.

"The guys who robbed St. Michael's," Hood said.

"Not much detail," she said. "Both wore ski masks. Both average build, one taller than the other. Taller guy, maybe five eleven, was the one who spoke. He kept one hand in his coat pocket like he might have a gun. Shorter guy, but not much shorter, snatched the cash box. Apparently, it happened pretty quick."

"Could be the same guys who hit the Trivia Night at Holy Family," Wally said.

"Could be," Hood agreed. "I'll take a look at both reports."

He returned to his office but, instead of comparing the reports from the church fundraisers, he reopened the Grace file and located the enclosed court docket, which tracked legal actions in the criminal case. The docket contained multiple entries from the prosecutor and public defender assigned to the case. Hood scanned to the end of the docket and read the entry: Convicted by jury of three lesser-included offenses of murder in the second degree, sentenced to three life sentences to be served concurrently, remanded to the custody of the Missouri Department of Corrections.

Hood was familiar enough with the judicial system to realize serving 29 years of a life term was not atypical, particularly if the inmate was a model prisoner, which Jacob apparently was. What Hood found difficult to understand was the jury's reduction of the charges from capital to second-degree murders.

He scanned the file and learned Jacob's public defender was Grant Ward, a legal wunderkind who had amassed stellar records as both a defender and a prosecutor before being elected as an associate circuit judge, the job he now held. Ward had built his successful defense on the premise that Jacob's killings were not premeditated but instead were one-time acts of unbridled passion. Hood found the outcome even more notable after reading that Jacob Grace never uttered a single word about the crimes and didn't assist in his own defense.

Also enclosed was a civil case docket, where Hood learned that the legal guardians appointed for Angela Grace were her maternal grandparents, Samuel and Luella Bunch, and that Jacob's assets, including the family farm, had been held in trust for Angela.

Hood sat back in his chair and considered the connection—Samuel and Luella Bunch were the parents of Ruth Bunch, the murdered spouse. And Ruth was a sister of Andrew Bunch, the father of Hood's rookie deputy John Bunch, nicknamed Young John.

He arose and returned to Maggie's station.

"I just found out," Hood said, "that Young John's grandparents were named guardians for Angela Grace after the massacre."

"I guess that's right," Maggie said, mentally tracing the connection. "Ruth was a Bunch before she married Jacob Grace, and the court awarded Ruth's parents custody of little Angela."

"Do you know if they're still alive?"

"The grandparents?" she asked. "I don't think so." When her boss failed to respond, Maggie added, "Want me to find out?"

Hood nodded. "If you would, please."

CHAPTER

6

Hood parked his cruiser in Angela Grace's driveway, careful not to block the immaculate silver BMW sedan he had not seen the previous day.

He climbed the porch steps and knocked. While he waited, he focused on what he guessed was the spot where Angela's mother had bled to death nearly three decades earlier.

The door opened. "Sheriff," Odessa said, her tone indicating surprise.

"I'd like to speak with Angela," he said. "And, no, I don't have an appointment."

"She's with someone."

Hood smiled. "I'll wait."

Odessa's body language suggested a combination of reluctance and annoyance. "I'll check," she said. "Wait here."

Hood almost expected her to close the door in his face, but she didn't. He was prepared, if asked, to say he was on a fact-finding visit, but he couldn't deny his curiosity had been piqued by Angela, her lifestyle, and her seeming contradictions.

His working theory was the assault on Jacob was

motivated by retribution for the murders, but, as he waited, he also considered the possibility that the attack was meant as a warning to Jacob to steer clear of Angela.

Odessa, he thought, seemed very protective of Angela. What, he wondered, was the relationship between the two women? How long had they known each other? Was their connection strictly employer and employee or more than that?

Odessa returned and said, "Let me show you to the parlor. Angela will be with you shortly."

As Hood followed, he saw a veiled Angela, Prince, and a man he didn't recognize emerge into the hallway. Hood veered toward them and extended his hand to the stranger. "Hello," he greeted. "I'm your sheriff, Francis Hood."

"A pleasure," the man said. He accepted the handshake. "I'm Ethan Diffenbaugh."

"I hope I'm not interrupting." Hood said, then smiled at Odessa, whose expression and posture suggested indignation.

"Not at all," Angela replied. "Ethan was just leaving."

"You look familiar," Hood said. "Have I seen you around the courthouse?" The question was a ruse. Nothing about the man's curly reddish hair or freckled complexion was familiar.

"I'm an attorney," Ethan said.

"Maybe that's it. Maybe I've seen you at the jail. Visiting a client, perhaps?"

"I should hope not, Sheriff." Ethan indulged in an abbreviated chuff. "Nothing about criminal law is appealing or lucrative."

"Ethan specializes in contract law," Angela interjected. "Now then," she added, addressing Ethan, "I mustn't keep the sheriff waiting."

While Odessa escorted Ethan to the front door, Hood preceded Angela and Prince into the parlor, where they settled in the places they had occupied the previous day. Although Prince seemed more relaxed, he remained standing.

"I think Prince wants to say hello," Angela said. "Do you mind?"

"Not at all. I like dogs."

She whispered a command to Prince, who walked to the sheriff and sniffed his hand. Prince didn't flinch when the sheriff extended his hand to pet him; after several strokes, the dog returned to his owner and sat.

"I'm surprised by your visit," Angela said. "I thought we had concluded our business."

"Well, yes and no. I was wondering if I could see some of your work."

"My work?"

Hood nodded. "I read you sometimes hide images in your illustrations. I wanted to see how that works. You know, see if I could find them or if you'd have to point them out for me."

"Where did you read that?"

"In an article I found online."

"Oh," she said, knowingly, "the *Artistry* article."

"That's the one."

"Don't believe everything you read, Sheriff."

"Are you saying that was wrong?"

"I'm saying I'm surprised you took the time and trouble to read an old magazine article about me."

"I'm interested."

"In my art?"

Hood splayed his fingers in a gesture that implied "Why not?"

"None of my finished pieces are kept here. All I have are some things I'm working on."

Hood shrugged. "That's okay."

"I'm afraid not," she said, her tone courteous, but firm. "I don't share unfinished pieces."

"The article also mentioned something about, I don't know, an ability to connect music and art."

"It's a neurological condition. It's called synesthesia."

"What's that like?"

"Forgive me, Sheriff," she said. She patted her dog's flank. "Prince likes you. I can tell. He senses you're here to help. But if I may be candid, I know you're not here as an art lover or budding neurologist; you're here because my father was attacked and family members typically are the most likely suspects. As the only surviving family member, and one with one hell of an axe to grind, I get why you're here."

Hood nodded slightly, not surprised by her insight.

"Well," Angela continued, "I can assure you I didn't do it, but you'd probably be more inclined to believe me if I had an alibi."

Again, Hood nodded.

"What time did it happen?"

SENSE OF GRACE

"Sometime between midnight and 3:30 a.m. yesterday."

"Then, no, I have no alibi. Odessa and I both turned in around ten and didn't see each other again until morning. We have separate bedrooms, by the way, despite some community speculation to the contrary, so she probably couldn't verify that I was here all night."

"And I'm guessing you can't verify she was."

Angela's gaze was cool. "Think what you like about me, but don't involve Odessa in this."

"Because?"

"Because she didn't do it. She wouldn't."

"You seem pretty confident—"

"It's not her nature, Sheriff."

"Then I'm back to square one," Hood mused aloud.

A brief silence ensued. "Are you a Christian, Sheriff?" Angela asked.

Hood was not prepared for the abrupt change of topic or the question. "I was raised in the Catholic tradition," he said.

"That's really not an answer."

"That's really not a question I'm asked very often."

"Please don't take it personally," she said, her tone apologetic. "I didn't mean to pry. It's just, I've been asked to illustrate a children's book introducing them to the major religions, and I'm at a loss about what to draw for the chapter on Christianity." She paused. "Jesus just seems so—what's the word?—uninspired."

Hood shrugged, still puzzled by her digression.

"Have you considered a random assault and robbery?"

she asked.

Hood's expression revealed confusion.

"The assault on my father," Angela clarified. "I mean, a man walking alone on a dark road in the early morning hours is a mugging waiting to happen."

"It's a possibility," Hood said, relieved the conversation had returned to his original topic, "but it doesn't explain cutting off an ear."

"Maybe they struggled."

"The ear is missing. We searched for it. Me and a couple EMTs looked for more than an hour and never found it. So I have to ask myself: Why would the assailant take the ear?"

She offered no response.

"Know what I think? I think it was a trophy, a prize for someone acting as an avenger or protector."

"Now you sound more like a therapist than a sheriff."

Hood shrugged. "I'm just trying to understand who I'm dealing with."

"Sheriff," Angela said, "since I was a child I've seen more therapists, counselors, psychologists, and psychiatrists than I can count. I've been tested, analyzed, and had my head examined so many times, my brain has more scar tissue than my body. I've been urged to remember and to forget, to heal and to move on. I don't have any special insight, empathy, or ability to deal with what happened or understand why." She paused and looked at the floor. "Mostly, I just want to live my life." She arose and added, "Now, if you'll excuse me."

Hood stood. "Thank you for your time."

SENSE OF GRACE

* * * * *

Hood turned from Angela's driveway onto Route AA and headed east. He slowed when he saw a large yellow Labrador Retriever sniffing the base of a roadside mailbox. He recognized the dog as Buster, then spotted the canine's owner, Clarence Jobe, ambling along the driveway toward the road.

Hood pulled onto the shoulder, stopped beside the mailbox, and lowered the passenger-side window. He called to Clarence, but it was Buster who put his front paws on the windowsill and peered into the cruiser's interior.

"Down Buster," Hood commanded.

Buster barked a friendly welcome and slobbered on the empty passenger seat.

"Buster get down," Clarence shouted. "You tryin' to get arrested?"

The dog obeyed.

"Sorry Sheriff," Clarence greeted. "Damned dog ain't got a lick of sense. What brings you out our way?"

"Just visiting with your neighbor, Angela."

"No trouble, I hope," Clarence said. Buster leaned penitently into his owner's leg, and Clarence patted the dog's flank.

"No. No trouble," Hood assured. He noticed the unmistakable touch of Father Time in the old farmer's features. Wrinkles creased Clarence's wizened face, and veins lined the backs of his arthritic hands. The Jobe property was one of

Huhman County's "Century Farms," a title bestowed on farms that had remained within the same family for a hundred years or more. Hood lamented that its days—like those of other farms in the county—were numbered. Clarence and wife, Mary Agnes, were childless and no extended family members were interested in accepting the uncertainties inherent in farming. "I'm guessing," Hood said, "you've known Angela all her life."

"Sure, 'cept those years when she was with her guardians, the Bunches," Clarence said. "We arranged with the court to farm the land 'til she was old enough to decide what to do with the property."

"You still farm it, don't you?"

"Yep. After she decided to move back into the house, we kept the arrangement."

"You see her much?"

"Not a lot. Mostly she keeps to herself, but sometimes when I'm out on the tractor, I see her painting in that big sunroom she had built on the back of the house. Sometimes she comes to the door when I go up there to pay my rent for the acreage, but mostly that other girl answers my knock."

"Odessa?"

"Yeah," Clarence said. He rubbed his chin. "I think that's her name. Short, dark hair?"

Hood nodded. "That's Odessa." He produced a card from his shirt pocket and handed it to Clarence. "If you hear or see anything out of the ordinary, let me know, okay?"

"Like what?"

"Anything."

"Anything could be anything," Clarence said. "Something I should know?"

"Her father's been released from prison. He got assaulted the other day on Old Cedar Creek Road."

Clarence rubbed his chin again. "I'll be damned," he said.

Hood slid into the restaurant booth opposite his wife Linda and daughter Elizabeth.

"So how's school?" he asked.

"Okay, I guess."

Any follow-up was interrupted by the fluttering of a teenage girl, only a year or two older than Elizabeth, who appeared beside their booth and said, "HelloI'mMandyand-I'llbeyourserver."

For Hood, her effervescent introduction seemed a protracted chirp.

"CanIstartyouwithsomethingtodrink?" Mandy continued as she distributed menus encased in plastic.

Linda and Elizabeth opted for iced tea. Hood said, "Water's fine."

Hood noticed Elizabeth silently mimic Mandy's words as the waitress departed. He purposely overlooked her mocking gesture. Instead, he asked, "How are your grades looking this semester?"

"Okay," Elizabeth said, concealing her face with the menu.

"Just okay?" he asked. Elizabeth seemed distant, almost

sullen. Linda had warned him their daughter was going through a freshman, little-fish-in-a-big-pond, trying-to-fit-in phase, but Hood—remembering Elizabeth's chatty middle-school years—wanted more than monosyllables. "How about extra-curricular—" he began.

"Hereweare," Mandy interrupted, alighting beside their table. "Two iced teas." She slowed the tempo of her speech to correspond with placement of the beverages. "And for you, sir, your water."

"Thanks."

"Readytoorder?" Mandy prompted.

Consensus was lacking. Linda had decided, Elizabeth wavered, and Hood inquired about the specials. Mandy's exuberance never waned. She seemed incapable of remaining still as she proudly parroted the memorized specials. When she had gathered their orders and retrieved the menus, she nearly sprinted to the kitchen.

"Talkabouthyper," Elizabeth mocked.

"Elizabeth," Linda scolded.

"How're the drill team practices going?" Hood asked his daughter.

Elizabeth focused on her place mat.

"She stopped doing that," Linda answered.

Hood hesitated momentarily. "Interfering with studies?"

"It's just lame. None of my friends are doing that anymore. Maybe they should ask perky Mandy to join."

Her response unsettled Hood. He sat back in the booth. He felt out of touch, as though he no longer recognized his daughter. He knew their bond had weakened during his drinking days, and now he wondered if the damage he had done could be repaired. Even his attempt at pleasant dinner conversation had faltered. He was thinking about how to proceed when he felt the vibration of his cell phone.

The readout indicated the call was from dispatch. "I'd better take this," he said. He excused himself, arose, and answered while he walked outside where the October air was chilly.

"Sorry to bother you," said Amber, the night-shift dispatcher, "but Young John didn't show up for his shift. You didn't leave any instructions about a fill-in, but I was wondering if you gave him some time off because of his accident."

"No. I was told it was just a fender bender. He didn't call in?"

"No," Amber said. "Want me to call him?"

"Are we short staffed?"

"Not really. It's been pretty quiet. Should I call him?"

"No," Hood said. "He might be feeling some aftereffects. Maybe he took something for the pain and nodded off. I'm at a restaurant not far from his house. I'll stop by on the way home."

"Okay. I'll call or text you if he shows up."

"Thanks." Hood broke the connection. He returned to the booth, where Elizabeth was busily texting and Linda was using a napkin to absorb condensation that had formed on the side of her iced tea glass.

"Emergency?" his wife asked.

"No, I'll deal with it after dinner." Hood slid into his seat. He was puzzled by Young John's behavior, which was atypical. He also was disconcerted by his daughter's preoccupation with texting during what he had envisioned as family time. Still, he said nothing.

When their meals were served, Elizabeth pocketed her phone and they all automatically folded their hands and bowed their heads while Linda said grace. She insisted on blessing every meal, and Hood appreciated the gesture. She never invited, cajoled, or coerced anyone else to do it. She simply offered a brief, spontaneous prayer. When Hood ate alone, he neglected the blessing.

The silence observed for grace lingered during the beginning of the meal. Hood feared that asking his daughter additional questions might be construed as an interrogation. He didn't want to make things worse.

Thankfully, Linda advanced the conversation, almost single-handedly. She posed rhetorical questions based on recent activities—"Guess who I ran into at the grocery store?" or, "Do you have any idea what it costs to dry clean a coat these days?"—then proceeded to answer them.

Hood intentionally ate unhurriedly, but when they all were finished, he promptly signaled Mandy for the check and paid the bill.

As he drove from the restaurant, alone, he felt somehow both relieved and troubled.

* * * * *

Modest might be the word a real estate agent would use to characterize Young John's home—a newer, single-story rancher with an attached, two-car garage. Hood guessed the floor plan included three bedrooms and one and a half baths, perhaps one and three quarters.

He rang the doorbell and waited. He was about to ring again when the door was opened by Young John's wife, Beth, who braced the couple's infant son William on her hip. "Sheriff," she said, her surprise apparent.

"Francis," he said, more an invitation than a correction. "Sorry to drop by unexpected. Is your husband home?"

She stepped outside, stood beside him on the concrete stoop and partially closed the door behind her. "Yes," she said, lowering her volume to half-whisper, "but he's not feeling well."

"From the accident?"

"Accident?"

Hood needed no detective skills to detect her surprise. "Well, I was told it was just a minor fender-bender."

Beth repositioned William higher on her hip but said nothing.

"I thought maybe he was in some pain and took something that made him drowsy," Hood continued. "It's just not like him to miss a shift without calling."

"Oh," she said. William began fussing, and she bounced him slightly on her hip.

"It's kind of chilly out here," Hood said. "Should we go inside and—?"

"No, no," she replied, cutting off his suggestion. "Let me just—I'll just—"

"Beff," Young John's voice called from within the house. "Who's 'at?"

Hood looked beyond Beth and into the living room, where Young John's staggering steps matched his slurred speech. He stopped, began to lose his balance and reached for the back of a recliner to steady himself. Hood's first thought was his deputy had suffered a concussion. "We need to help him," he said as he brushed past Beth and entered the living room. He steadied his deputy and realized immediately the cause of the stupor was not a concussion: it was intoxication. Young John reeked of alcohol.

"It's not what you think," said Beth, who had followed the sheriff inside.

"I'm going to put him to bed," Hood said. "Which room?"

With Beth as his guide, Hood assisted Young John along a hallway and into bed. The deputy closed his eyes and, within moments, began snoring.

Hood returned to the front door, again followed by Beth, who continued to clutch William and apologize in sentence fragments—"He never does this," "I hope you don't think," "I mean, this isn't—"

Hood pulled open the door. "Have him call me tomorrow."

"Tomorrow," she repeated.

In her expression, Hood saw fear and uncertainty about what tomorrow might bring. He looked at the infant, who offered only a blank stare.

INTERLUDE:

Jesus Loves Me

Amazing Grace!

How sweet the sound . . .

The melody is in Angela's head, a sound so sweet she can almost see it.

She is mulling ideas for the new children's book she has been commissioned to illustrate. The book is intended as an age-appropriate overview of the major religions, not a devotional for a specific denomination.

Angela remembers her mother repeatedly would sing "Amazing Grace" as a lullaby intended to quiet her daughter. Angela knows her mother's old phonograph and the record album that includes the Christian hymn are stored in the attic. She knows because she put them there.

She has no difficulty finding them. Years ago, she sorted, catalogued, and stored everything that belonged to her mother and her two brothers.

Angela retrieves the record and phonograph and carries them to her sunlit studio. She feels the anticipation of having a starting point. Angela does not consider herself religious, although her mother raised her as a Catholic and routinely brought her daughter to Sunday mass. Angela once asked why her father didn't attend and was told adults get to make their own choices. After the massacre, she continued attending mass with her guardians, also Catholics, but when she became an adult, she made the choice to abandon the church.

In the studio, she unlatches the hinges of the phonograph and repositions its lid, which also serves as a stereo speaker. She opens her drawing pad to a blank page and gathers the colored pencils she intends to use for the sketch, then gently places the phonograph needle on the first song.

Amazing Grace!
How sweet the sound, that saved a wretch like me!
I once was lost, but now am found,
Was blind, but now I see.

She listens to the lyrics but sees no images.
Nothing.
When the song ends, she lifts the needle.
She is troubled now. She senses nothing.
She replaces the needle and plays the song again.
Nothing.
The song ends; another begins.

SENSE OF GRACE

> Jesus loves me! This I know.
> For the Bible tells me so.
> Little ones to him belong.
> They are weak, but He is strong.
> Yes, Jesus loves me!
> Yes, Jesus loves me!
> Yes, Jesus loves me!
> The Bible tells me so.

Prompted by the lyrics, the notes, and the melody, she sketches a series of lines—primarily in light blues and reds—on the pad. Her hand works almost feverishly, as if trying to keep pace with the tempo.

> Jesus loves me! He who died,
> Heaven's gate is open wide.

Angela stops drawing. She stops the record. *Heaven's gate.* Why a gate? The image in her mind baffles her. A gate provides, but also restricts, entry. She wonders whether to draw the gate open or closed. She replaces the phonograph needle and hears the reassuring couplet:

> He will wash away my sin,
> That His child may enter in.

Again, her hand is moving, letting the song fill her senses and direct her drawing.

Jesus loves me! He will stay
Close beside me all the way;
If I trust Him, when I die
He will take me home on high.

The song ends. Angela knows she will play it again; she will play it repeatedly until she captures the image it is conveying to her. She looks at what she has sketched so far. She has drawn not one child at the gate, but two. And neither of them is a girl. Although they are faceless and indistinct, she recognizes them as Brian and David, her brothers.

CHAPTER

7

"Good morning," Maggie greeted.

"Morning," Hood said as he bee-lined to the coffee maker.

"Young John was here when I got here," Maggie told her boss, as he filled a disposable cup. She lowered her volume to a whisper. "I think he wants to see you."

Hood nodded. He wasn't surprised; he suspected his rookie deputy was worried. Hood wasn't inclined to keep him waiting, so he walked directly to his own office. As he passed Young John's desk, he motioned for his deputy to follow. Once inside, Hood said, "Close the door. Have a seat." He had experienced enough hangovers of his own to recognize the one visible on his deputy's face. "How're you feeling?"

"Been better. Look, about last night, I don't know what got into me, but it won't happen again."

Hood remained silent for a moment, then said, "John, you've got an excellent record. No tardiness, no complaints about your performance, and until yesterday, no unexcused absences. You've been a model employee. So when something like this happens, I've got to think there's a reason. I'm not here to discipline or punish you, I'm here to understand what's going on."

Young John shrugged. "Nothing. It's fine," he said, his tone unconvincing.

"If there *is* something, it's better I hear it from you and not someone else."

The deputy scanned the familiar surroundings of the office. Hood waited patiently.

"You know," Young John said, "things just kind of get overwhelming sometimes. There's the house and the bills and the baby, and Beth's on maternity leave so money is kind of tight right now. I'm trying, I'm really trying to keep up with everything, you know, but . . . "

"How can I help?" Hood asked. "Do you need some time off?"

"No," Young John replied. "That's the last thing I need. I mean, I need the money and, plus, being here helps take my mind off that other stuff."

Hood thought about "that other stuff"—what his program of recovery characterized as "life on life's terms"—earning a living, raising children, paying bills, adapting to changing circumstances. Initially, Hood drank to seek relief from, or to numb himself to, life's challenges. Eventually, his drinking morphed into alcoholism, and he didn't need a reason. He wondered if Young John was starting on a similar path.

"I'm fine, really," Young John said. "I'm really sorry about missing my shift and not calling. I really am. But it won't happen again. I promise."

Hood considered the words. "Okay."

"Thanks."

Hood leaned forward and scanned a document on his desktop. "By the way, 'Sweeps Week' starts tomorrow," he said, referring to the round of simultaneous drug raids coordinated by the Mid-Missouri Drug Task Force. The operation included dozens of officers from the state highway patrol, county sheriffs', and municipal police departments. Officers worked in pairs and carried warrants for the arrests of known drug dealers. Hood was a Sweeps Week veteran; for Young John, it would be a new experience.

"I'd like you to pair up with me," Hood said. "The briefing is at 6 a.m. tomorrow in the patrol's assembly room. We'll get addresses and last-minute instructions before we head out. You okay with that?"

"Of course."

"Good. I'm counting on you."

"Breakfast? Are you kidding?" Jet asked.

"We gotta switch it up some," Randy replied. "'Til now, we been doing church events at night. Cops see a pattern and they react to that." The two sat together in the Cutlass parked in a corner of the lot at St. Aloysius School.

"This *is* a church," Jet said. "My mom used to say there's a special place in Hell for people who take from a church."

"Technically, it's a school connected to the church," Randy argued. He worked the toothpick between his lower bicuspids. "And this pancake breakfast thing is for some private youth art group that just meets here, so it's really two steps away from being a church function."

"How much coin we lookin' at?"

"No idea," Randy said. "That's why I'm going to scope it out first. I'll take a look at the cash box, the layout, and—if it looks good—I'll come back, put on my coveralls, and we'll do it."

Jet shook his head. "Keep messin' with God, man," he muttered.

"Don't you worry about God," Randy said. He shouldered the driver's door open and spat the toothpick on the ground. "He's got bigger things to deal with—wars and shit."

Randy crossed the parking lot and pushed through the rear doors. The ground-floor gymnasium where the event was being held was directly to his right. He peered through the open doorway into the gym and assessed the two lines of people—one for ticket holders and another to purchase tickets—the breakfast buffet, and the arrangement of folding tables and chairs.

The ticket sellers and cash box were in the populated gym rather than in the quieter hallway, Randy noted, as he joined the line to purchase tickets. He was peeking in the cash box and contemplating whether a snatch-and-go would succeed when a voice from nearby said, "Randy?"

He turned and saw the tall, sleek figure of a woman dressed in black pants and a white turtleneck accented by a vest with yellow and red geometric shapes. Her daffodil-blonde hair was straight and long, and she gazed at him with bright, silver-blue eyes. The remainder of her face was hidden by an opaque veil.

Synapses fired in the deep recesses of Randy's memory as he constructed an image of a friend he hadn't seen since childhood. "Angela?" he ventured.

She nodded. "I thought it might be you, but it's been—" She stopped. "How long has it been?"

"We were kids," he answered. "My gosh. I can't believe it's you."

She extended her arms, Randy lifted his hands—one covered with a mitten—and they hugged awkwardly. For Angela, the gesture was spontaneous and uncharacteristic, motivated by a surge of fond memories for the only boy— indeed, the only student—who didn't avoid her in the wake of the killings. If anything, circumstances had brought them closer—two children taunted and belittled because they were different.

"I had no idea you were in town," Angela said. "The last I knew, you and your mom—"

"I just got back a few days ago."

"Here, let me give you a complementary ticket. This event is for a charity I started. It's called Helping Children Through Art." She reached into her vest pocket and handed him a ticket. "Need another? Are you by yourself?"

"Yeah. I mean no. I don't need another ticket."

"Are you back here visiting your dad?"

"No. Not exactly."

"No matter," Angela said. "It's good to see you. I mean, what are the odds we would meet again here—at my fundraiser, of all places—after all these years?"

The irony flashed in Randy's mind, coupled with the realization the robbery was off.

"I'd love to sit and chat," Angela said, "but I've got to do the meet-and-greet thing."

Randy improvised. "I was just getting a to-go box anyway."

"But we've got to get together, get reacquainted. Here's my card," she said, producing a business card from a separate vest pocket. "Call me."

"I will."

"Really, I mean it," she said. "You were my only friend from back then. You're special. Promise you'll call."

"I promise."

Hood hated free time.

Keeping busy was his way of avoiding thoughts—including rationalizations, justifications, and temptations. He had about a half hour to kill, enough time at least to begin comparing the robbery reports from the Holy Family Catholic Church Trivia Night and St. Michael's Sodality Sale-A-Rama. He retrieved them from a stack of paperwork and reread both, concentrating on the similarities. Both were sponsored by Catholic charitable groups, and both were held in the evening at church-owned facilities. In both, the suspects wore ski masks and gloves; although one suspect suggested he was armed, no weapon was displayed. Suspect descriptions from witnesses were vague and, at times, contradictory. The consensus was both were male—one white, one black—of average height and weight, with no distinguishing characteristics. One of the Sale-A-Rama witnesses described the suspect vehicle as a "beat up" dark sedan, but no one knew the make or model. Its license plates were missing.

Or, Hood thought, intentionally removed. Comparing the reports didn't solidify a connection, but Hood found the similarities more than coincidental.

Although he was reluctant to give credit to criminals, he had to admit the robberies reflected a degree of ingenuity. Robbing businesses—from banks to convenience stores—is risky. Cameras record activities, alarms may be triggered, and employees are trained to gather identifying information. But church groups rarely take such precautions because they don't expect to be robbed. They should, Hood thought, because they are comparatively easier targets. They collect cash, often in large amounts, at a single, unsecured location tended only by one or two volunteers, often senior members, who have probably never before witnessed a crime.

As Hood contemplated what kind of person was clever enough, yet despicable enough, to rob a charity, he glanced at the clock. Time to go.

* * * * *

Ethan Diffenbaugh, attorney at law, was not difficult to find. His self-promotion in the newspaper and on television featured his face, phone number, and downtown office building address.

Hood was greeted by a receptionist and directed to take a seat in an otherwise empty waiting room. He sat beside an artificial fern and was kept waiting long enough to suggest the attorney was a busy man.

The office he eventually entered was decorated to impress—an ensemble of cherry furnishings, leather upholstery, and brass accessories.

"Thanks for seeing me so quickly. I know your time is valuable," Hood said, purposely ingratiating himself. He sat in one of the client chairs facing Ethan's desk.

"Of course," said Ethan, who had perched in a high-back desk chair elevating him slightly above the eye level of visitors.

"I'm here because of Angela. Well, actually because of what happened to her father."

Ethan said nothing.

"Did Angela tell you her father was assaulted?"

"Yes," Ethan replied. "I didn't even know he'd been released until she told me about your conversation. Said someone cut off his ear."

"Yes," Hood affirmed.

Ethan again was silent, as if evaluating his response. "So what's that got to do with me?"

"I was wondering if you might have any idea who assaulted him."

"None."

"Have you known Angela a long time?"

Ethan leaned forward and folded his hands atop his desk. "Sheriff, I'm Angela's attorney and adviser, and at times I act as her agent. As I'm sure you know, attorney-client privilege requires—"

"I'm just asking how long you've known her."

"Why?"

"Well, Angela is kind of an, I don't know . . . " Hood shrugged, allowing the sentence to lapse into silence.

"I think the word you're looking for," Ethan said, "is enigma."

Hood feigned ignorance of the word. "Enigma," he repeated. "What's that mean exactly?"

"She's not easy to figure out. She's a mystery, a puzzle."

"That's it," Hood said. "I'm just trying to figure out why she stays here. Especially in that house—after what happened. I mean, she's so successful now."

"She doesn't like the limelight," Ethan said. "Don't get me wrong—she's not a recluse. She understands that premieres and galas at exhibitions and galleries are part of the business. But she's not like other artists; she'd rather skip all that. She'd rather speak through her art than gab with art critics or cultivate the well-heeled at pretentious parties."

Hood was encouraged by Ethan's candor. "I'm also kind of fuzzy about Odessa and what she does."

"Odessa," Ethan said, an unmistakable hint of derision in his tone. "Angela took her in. That all happened a long time ago. Before I came into the picture."

"What do you mean—took her in?"

"Talk about an enigma; Odessa's the poster child. She was abandoned as an infant. Some firefighters heard her cries and found her outside the station. No note, no birth certificate, no nothing. That was in the city of Odessa, so the firemen started calling her that, and it stuck. She was in and out of foster care, lived on the streets, got into all kinds of trouble. Finally, a family here took her in and enrolled her in Helping Children Through Art; that's an art school Angela operates. They met there and, somehow, they connected. When Odessa aged out of the foster system, Angela invited her to move in."

"In what capacity?"

"I don't know, exactly," Ethan said. "I mean, she maintains the house and yard—and she does a heck of a job, I'll give her that—but she's always getting involved in other areas."

"Other areas?"

"Okay, first she learned how to frame art and package it for shipment—which is fine, it saves money. But, now, she's becoming more involved in deciding what pieces Angela should include in an exhibit and also what invitations Angela should accept or reject."

Hood sensed resentment in Ethan's tone. "How do you and Odessa get along?"

"Fine," Ethan said, without conviction.

"Because I can see how if I was somebody's attorney and

adviser, and someone else started to interfere—"

"What are you trying to imply?" Ethan asked.

"Nothing. I'm just trying to understand—"

"I've already said more than I should," Ethan interrupted. "I know why you're here, Sheriff, and it's not to understand. It's to try to find out who attacked Angela's father. And I'm aware that my client and the people around her are prime suspects. Am I right?"

Hood produced a crooked frown; again, his motives had been uncovered. "I haven't ruled out any—"

"Well you can rule out Angela and me. I didn't do it, and neither did she. I know her too well."

"And Odessa?"

"I can't speak for Odessa." Ethan stiffened, indicating the conversation was over.

"Thank you for your time," Hood said. He left.

Ethan, Hood thought, had been much more forthcoming about Odessa than about Angela. Admittedly, Odessa wasn't his client, but Ethan's reticence regarding Angela seemed based on something more.

Hood decided to visit Angela again. After all, he was out and about, her farm was only minutes away, and he could provide a progress report, although he had little progress to report.

No vehicles were in Angela's driveway when he parked, but he spotted Odessa in the front yard using a power sweeper to herd leaves into piles. As he exited his cruiser, Odessa switched off the machine and informed him Angela hadn't returned home from a breakfast fundraiser she had hosted on behalf of her charity. Odessa was curt, but no more than on previous visits. Hood believed her.

He left, traveled eastbound on Route AA and, when the Jobe property came into view, turned into the driveway. Before he came to a complete stop, Buster, the yellow Lab, trotted to the cruiser and sat beside the driver's door.

Hood powered down the window. "Hey, Buster, you need to give me room to get out." Buster wagged his tail, panted and slobbered, but didn't budge. Hood cracked the door open and used it to nudge the dog—gently. If anything, Buster seemed to lean into the door with greater resistance.

While Hood contemplated his predicament, Mary Agnes opened the storm door facing the driveway.

"Morning, Sheriff," she greeted. She wiped her hands on a dishtowel. "Thought I heard someone drive up."

"Morning," Hood called through the open window. "Old Buster here would make a good police dog. He's got me trapped."

Mary Agnes laughed. Although she was a small woman, her laugh—like her voice—was sonorous. "Buster, come over here, or I'll jerk a knot in your tail." The dog stood and loped to her side, where he sat and leaned against her leg.

"Clarence here?" Hood asked. He got out of the cruiser and stretched.

"Out in the shop, I think."

Hood surveyed the cluster of outbuildings.

"There," Mary Agnes said, pointing to a single-story structure with three overhead doors.

"I was hoping to talk with you both."

"Tell 'im to take a break then," she said. "The old man works too damned hard anyway. I'll put on some fresh coffee."

"I don't want you to go to any trouble."

"No trouble. Tell 'im I just took some fresh biscuits out of the oven. That'll get 'im in here."

Hood walked to the shop and peered through a glass pane in one of the doors. A bright work light illuminated Clarence, who was seated on a stool using a file to sharpen a mower blade locked in a vice.

Hood tapped on the window.

Apparently startled by the sound, Clarence looked up and, seeing his visitor, nodded in recognition. He put down the file and came out through a side door.

"Morning Clarence."

"Morning. What brings you out here? I don't see you for months and now twice this week."

"Wanted to visit with you and Mary Agnes. She said to tell you she's got fresh coffee and warm biscuits."

"Then what are we waiting for?"

In the kitchen, Hood placed his hat on an empty chair and sat at the table perpendicular to Clarence. Mary Agnes distributed plates, with a basket of biscuits wrapped in the folds of a gingham cloth, a tub of butter, and an assortment of homemade jams. She set a steaming mug of coffee before each man, then cradled a mug of her own in her hands while she leaned against the counter.

Hood considered inviting her to join them at the table but didn't. He knew Mary Agnes adhered to the tradition of remaining ready to serve family and guests. Near her feet, Buster traced the perimeter of a braided, oval rug several times before curling himself into a ball.

"I'm not sure exactly how to start," Hood said. "I've been reading the file about what happened at the Grace farm back in—"

"That was a long time ago," Clarence said. "Why do you want to bring that back up?" He spread blackberry jam on a biscuit, took a large bite and chewed.

Hood hesitated. "Well, like I told you the other day, Jacob Grace was assaulted on Old Cedar Creek Road not far from here."

"Dear me," Mary Agnes said with obvious surprise.

Hood guessed Clarence hadn't shared the information with his wife. "It happened sometime between midnight Thursday and about 3 a.m. Friday morning. Did either of you hear anything?"

"Nope," Clarence said.

"We don't stay up that late," Mary Agnes added.

Hood nodded. "Anyway, I started reading the file about the, you know, incident that happened way back then. The report said you called the sheriff's department because you heard screams."

"Horrible screams," Mary Agnes said.

"That wasn't midnight, though," Clarence said. "It was earlier."

"Around 10:30, according to the report," Hood said.

"We were younger then," Mary Agnes said. "Much younger."

Again, Hood nodded. "Do you remember anything before the screaming started? Any commotion, a vehicle coming or going, anything?"

Clarence shook his head.

"In those days, it was usually pretty quiet out here," Mary Agnes said. "But those screams . . . " She let the remark dissolve into silence.

"Was the screaming constant or did it start and stop? Could you tell if it was coming from more than one person, both an adult and children?"

The Jobes looked at each other, not in a way that suggested a conspiracy, but rather a shared reluctance to recall the experience.

"At first I thought it was a fox," Clarence said. "Ever heard foxes cry when it's mating season?"

Hood shook his head.

"Sounds like torture," Clarence said.

"I don't know what I thought," Mary Agnes added. "I told Clarence to go on up there, and I called Sheriff Westerman. Got the dispatcher and told her they needed to send somebody to the Grace farm right away."

Hood faced Clarence, who sipped coffee. "What did you

see when you arrived?"

Clarence grimaced. "The screams had stopped. Ruth was lying on the porch." His lips began to quiver and he stopped, obviously distressed.

Hood waited.

"She was bleeding a lot," Clarence continued. "I tried to stop it but couldn't." His eyes were vacant, like he was someplace else. "So many wounds," he whispered. "So much blood."

"Sheriff," Mary Agnes said.

Hood nodded to signal he understood her plea for him to stop. "Just another question or two?"

"Let's get it done," Clarence said.

"Did you hear anything from inside the house? Did you go inside?"

"No. The deputies showed up, then Sheriff Westerman, then the ambulance people. They went in and brought out Jacob and little Angela."

"Must have come as quite a shock," Hood said, addressing Clarence. "I mean, your family and the Graces have lived next door to each other for generations."

"I still have a hard time believing it. Jacob was two or three years behind me in school, so we didn't spend much time together as kids, but I knew him as a neighbor." He paused. "Jacob was a hard man, sheriff. No doubt about that. But I never knew him to be evil—not until what he did to Ruth and those kids. Now that was evil."

A brief silence ensued before Hood asked, "Either of you

have any thoughts on who might have assaulted him?"

"Half the county probably would like to," Clarence said, "but to answer your question, I've got no idea."

Hood looked to Mary Agnes, who said, "I just feel bad for Angela. I thought all this was in the past."

Hood stood and picked up his hat. "Sorry to dredge it back up. I appreciate your help and your hospitality."

CHAPTER

8

Hood clutched the white cardboard bakery box as if it contained an unstable explosive.

He approached the door of Otto and Sarah Kampeters' home, which had become the refuge for his wife and daughter.

Linda had invited him to dinner—or, as she characterized it, a "little family gathering." Although he was appreciative, he also was a little annoyed. Invitations were for guests; he thought of himself as family. But as he stood at the door, he pictured himself holding the bakery box, something a guest would bring. He knocked.

"Francis," Linda's sister greeted him as she opened the door.

"Hi Sarah." He extended the box toward her. "This is for you."

"How nice, but you really didn't have to."

"It's a pie. From Millie's Diner. It's blueberry, Linda's favorite."

"How thoughtful." She stepped back. "Come in."

As he crossed the threshold into the kitchen, Sarah said,

"Francis is here. He brought a blueberry pie. From Millie's."

Sarah's announcement struck Hood as both theatrical and unnecessary. The only other people in the room were Otto and Linda, who were standing near the round oak kitchen table. Hood circled the table, and his wife greeted him with a delicate kiss, followed by Otto exuberantly pumping his hand.

Hood exchanged small talk while glancing at the kitchen archway, anticipating the arrival of his daughter. When she failed to appear, he asked, "Where's Elizabeth?"

"She's having dinner at a friend's house," Linda said.

Hood was disappointed to hear she would be absent from the "little family gathering." He wondered if it was another consequence of his alcoholism.

"So," Linda continued, addressing her husband. "How's work? Did you find out who cut that fellow's ear off the other day?"

"Ick," Sarah remarked, as she stood at the stove and stirred gravy then called. "Dinner's ready. Everyone, sit."

As Sarah served the meal—a large roast with red potatoes, cooked carrots, and celery—Hood outlined the investigation, including a brief background of Jacob Grace and a narrative of his encounters with Angela Grace.

"She sounds fascinating," Sarah said.

Hood was bothered by her remark, which seemed to insinuate he was fascinated by the artist. Without averting his gaze from Sarah, he asked, "So what's new with you?"

Including Linda and Otto with occasional glances, Sarah described a change in her duties at the state Social Services agency, a move she characterized as lateral rather than upward. She added she had agreed to serve as a district delegate for her recovery group, where, Hood knew, she was a nine-year member. "So," she concluded, turning to Hood, "How's your recovery going?"

He had anticipated the question would come up at some point during the evening. "Okay, I guess. I'm not drinking."

"Good." Sarah nodded repeatedly, a gesture Hood found condescending. "That's good, but there's a lot more to it than that. What's your program of recovery?"

Hood looked from Sarah to Linda, who seemed sympathetic to his discomfort with the interrogation but also interested in his answer. "I don't know that I have a program."

Obviously dissatisfied, Sarah persisted. "You go to meetings, right?"

"I go to Matthew's meeting," Hood said, hoping to mask his increasing irritation.

"And he's your sponsor, right?"

"Yes."

"What about service work? Have you thought about chairing a meeting?"

"Matthew runs the meeting."

"But there are other meetings where people can sign up to chair. Have you thought about going to other meetings?"

The question rekindled Hood's fear of maintaining anonymity in recovery. "No."

Sarah sat back in her chair. "I know you've admitted you're an alcoholic, but have you accepted you can't recover on your own, that you need to have faith in a power greater than you?"

Hood again glanced to Linda, then back at Sarah. What he saw was not one alcoholic trying to help another, but a sister-in-law trying to decide if he had earned the right to a reconciliation with Linda. He reached for his cell phone—which hadn't sounded or vibrated—and checked the blank screen. "Excuse me. I better take this," he lied.

He went outdoors and scrolled to Matthew's name on his phone contact list. Although his finger hovered above the number, he didn't press it. Instead, he went back inside where Sarah, Otto, and Linda were finishing dinner.

"Something's come up," he said. "I gotta go."

"Emergency?" Linda asked.

"Just something I need to take care of." He sensed Linda's disappointment as he lightly kissed her on the cheek, then thanked his hosts for dinner. "Sorry I couldn't stay longer," he said, feigning sincerity before he fled.

The lighted sign in the window of Good Times Liquor Store read "Open."

Hood sat in his vehicle in the parking lot. He alternated his focus between the sign and Matthew's contact number on the lighted screen of his cell phone.

Getting out of his vehicle, he walked toward the store, stopped, circled back, and tapped the number.

"Hello," Matthew answered.

"This is Francis. Am I calling at a bad time?"

"Not at all."

Silence followed.

"Everything okay, Francis?" Matthew asked.

Hood snorted a self-deprecating laugh. "I've been better."

"Where are you?"

"The Good Times parking lot."

"That's not a good place to be. You know that, right?"

"I guess. I probably wouldn't have called you otherwise."

"So let's meet somewhere. Okay?"

"Okay," Hood said. "How about Millie's Diner?"

"Great," Matthew said. "Why don't you head there now? Order me a decaf, and I'll be there shortly."

Hood ended the conversation and drove to Millie's. The dinner crowd had dispersed, leaving a smattering of customers. Hood sat in a secluded booth and ordered two coffees, a regular and a decaf.

The waitress delivered the order only moments before Matthew arrived. He wore a yellow sweatshirt and white painter's pants, both stained with a spectrum of dried paints. He slid onto the bench across from Hood.

"I did call at a bad time." Hood gestured at Matthew's color-blotched ensemble, which reminded Hood he was procrastinating on a painting project of his own.

"Not at all," Matthew said. "You called at the right time. I needed a break."

"I have a feeling you'd say that if I called at 3 a.m."

Matthew shrugged. "Maybe on that occasion 3 a.m.

would be the right time. So tell me—what got you to the Good Times parking lot?"

Hood sipped coffee. "Oddly enough, I was talking with another alcoholic. It didn't go well." He looked up at Matthew, who only nodded, encouraging him to continue. "Since my wife and daughter left, they've been staying with Linda's sister Sarah, who I think you know from the program."

"Sarah K."

Hood nodded.

"Sure," Matthew said. "She's been involved for, let's see, probably about a decade now."

"Nine years," Hood said. "Well, when I was drinking, my wife turned to Sarah for some answers and some help and, eventually, a place to stay."

"Go on."

"So, I was invited over there for dinner tonight, and Sarah started quizzing me about what she called my program of recovery. She just wouldn't let up. It was like she was trying to see if I was worthy, or would ever be worthy, to get back together with Linda." Hood rotated his cup on the tabletop. "I just kind of felt, I don't know—"

"Resentments can be—" Matthew began.

"I knew you were going to bring up resentments," Hood interrupted. "I know the program talks about resentments. But am I wrong?"

"Right and wrong have nothing to do with it," Matthew said. "There are justified resentments and unjustified resentments, but both of them can put me in the Good Times parking lot—or worse. For me, I have to get out of myself and see my behavior from the other person's perspective."

"I'm trying," Hood said. He reconsidered. "Now that I think about it, I may have been a little defensive tonight. I was on edge before I sat down." He rubbed his head. "I'm trying to change."

"And that's good," Matthew said. "Recovery changed me, but I didn't realize right away that the people around me also were changing, and I needed to give them the time and space to do that. I didn't become an alcoholic overnight, so when I quit drinking, I couldn't expect to earn their trust overnight. Recovery is a process."

"So," Hood said, "you think I should cut Sarah some more slack?"

"My life goes better when I cut everybody more slack."

Hood sipped coffee and contemplated Matthew's words. After a few moments, he said, "Sarah also questioned my faith."

"What did she say, exactly?"

"Something about I need to have faith in a higher power."

"I'm always encouraging alcoholics to do that. It worked for me. Do you know why that bothered you?"

"Maybe."

Matthew cocked his head, inviting Hood to elaborate.

"Maybe because . . . because since Linda and Elizabeth left, I've been having more doubts."

"Doubts don't necessarily mean a lack of faith," Matthew said. "I believe in a higher power, but I still have doubts."

Hood's expression revealed he was baffled.

"When I first got in the program," Matthew said, "all I had were doubts. I was one of those seeing-is-believing types. The people in recovery talked a lot about a higher power, but nobody forced their beliefs on me. They simply suggested I remain open to the possibility. At first, I rationalized a higher power—like what Mac shared at the meeting the other night. I figured if I couldn't quit drinking on my own but I wasn't drinking, something else must be at work. That was the beginning of a process for me. Over time, things have become much clearer."

Hood rubbed his scalp. "Right now," he said, "nothing is clear to me."

"Patience, my friend."

CHAPTER

9

Hood watched Young John during the early-morning "Sweeps Week" briefing and wondered if his deputy was suffering the same pre-drug raid anxiety he himself had experienced as a rookie.

Coordinated by the Mid-Missouri Drug Task Force, dozens of officers from the state highway patrol, county sheriffs', and municipal police departments conducted simultaneous drug raids in five Central Missouri counties. Working in pairs, each duo was issued the name, address, and arrest warrant for a known drug dealer.

When the briefing ended, Hood asked, "You okay?"

"Yeah," Young John answered as they arose from their seats. "Why?"

"You look a little, I don't know, pale," Hood said, his comment competing with the clattering of folding chairs being collapsed and loaded on carts.

"I'm fine."

A dismal morning drizzle shadowed them as they exited the building and made their way to the cruiser.

SENSE OF GRACE

Hood ratcheted the wiper blades between intermittent and normal as they drove to their assigned destination, a public housing complex officially named the Harris-Koechner Apartments and unofficially known as the "Projects." The housing units were configured like children's building blocks, abutted and stacked without adornment or imagination.

Hood knew the suspect, a mid-level drug dealer named Joey Trammel. Hood had busted him twice, with both arrests resulting in a reduction of charges from felony sales to misdemeanor possession.

The rain had let up by the time they arrived in the parking lot. Hood glanced at his partner, who looked as washed-out as the ashen morning light. "You sure you're all right? You don't look so good."

"I'm fine," Young John insisted. "Let's just do this." He opened the door and, as they had planned in advance, scrambled around Building C and peeked through the sliding-glass door of the ground-level apartment.

Hood entered the building's front door and walked along the hallway, inhaling a cloying combination of pine air freshener and urine. He stopped at the designated apartment, turned toward the microphone clipped to his shoulder, and whispered to his partner. "See anything?"

"No activity," Young John's disembodied voice said.

Hood rapped on the metal door. He waited, rapped again.

"I see him," Young John said. "No apparent weapon. He's in his skivvies."

A voice from within the apartment called out, "Who is it?"

RICHARD F. MCGONEGAL

"Huhman County Sheriff's Department."

"What d'ya want?"

"Joey, it's your sheriff, Francis Hood. Open up."

"Wait a minute."

Hood waited, then whispered into his microphone, "What's he doing, John?"

"Pacing—like he can't make up his mind." He paused. "Wait, he's heading for the door."

When Hood heard the sound of the door being unlocked, he pushed it open, gun leveled at Joey, who raised his arms and backed up. "On your knees," Hood commanded. When Joey obeyed, Hood added, "Now, on your belly, hands stretched out, palms on the floor."

"What's this all about?" Joey asked, prone on the soiled carpet.

"You're under arrest." Hood sidled to the sliding door and unlatched it.

"For what?" Joey asked.

"I'll ask the questions," Hood said, as Young John stepped into the apartment. "Anybody else here?"

"Man, you can't just come into my—"

"Stinks in here," Young John interrupted.

Hood holstered his sidearm, produced his handcuffs, and knelt beside Joey. "Check the bedroom," he instructed Young John.

"I'm gonna heave," his deputy said. He rushed the few steps into the filthy kitchenette, leaned over a sink piled with dirty dishes, and vomited.

The retching sound was smothered by a shout from a female voice. "Put your fuckin' hands up. Now. Both of you."

Hood and Young John immediately swiveled their heads and faced the woman who had emerged from the bedroom.

A casting director for a low-budget zombie movie would have signed her on the spot. Her skin was stretched and taut around deep eye sockets and prominent cheek bones, and her thin, pallid lips revealed a disarray of clenched teeth. More menacing than her facial features was the shotgun she pointed alternately at Hood and Young John. Both men observed that although her hands trembled and the gunstock was not braced against her shoulder, her finger circled the trigger.

"Okay," Hood said, adopting a calming tone. "Let's not . . . "

"Stay on your knees," she shouted at the sheriff. She pointed the gun at Young John. "You. Get over here and kneel next to him."

Young John obeyed.

"Get their guns, Joey," she hollered to him as he scrambled to his feet.

"I dunno, Cindy," Joey said. "Maybe . . . "

"I'm not doin' no more time," she said. "Grab their guns and radios, get some fuckin' pants on, and let's get out of here."

Joey hesitated, obviously undecided.

"You gonna make me shoot 'em so you can take your fuckin' time?"

"Shit," Joey said. He collected the guns and radios and disappeared into the bedroom.

Moments passed. No one moved or spoke.

Hood focused on Cindy, who appeared fixated on a strand of spittle, drool, or vomit, that slid from the corner of Young John's mouth to his chin, where it hung suspended. Young John seemed to look beyond her at a faded blue, one-armed armchair, as if trying to decide how it got that way.

Hood returned his attention to Cindy and her trembling hands. "Cindy," he said soothingly, as if willing her to ease the tension on her trigger finger, "you really don't want—"

"Don't," she shouted, as she swung the shotgun barrel to point at Hood's face. "Don't even fuckin' tell me what I want."

"We're not even here for you," Hood said. "We have an arrest warrant for Joey."

"Shut up. Joey, let's go."

Joey reappeared, clutching a bulging duffel bag.

"Okay," Cindy said. "Now we're all goin' to the kitchen." To Joey, she added, "Put those cuffs through the refrigerator door handle and cuff one guy on each side."

After Joey and Cindy left, Hood had to admit he was impressed by Cindy's impromptu ingenuity. And despite his predicament, he was happy at that moment just to be alive.

After they failed to report, Hood and Young John eventually were found and freed by other task force members. A subsequent radio dispatch resulted in the arrests of Joey and Cindy, as well as the recovery of the officers' guns and radios.

Enduring teasing and taunting from their peers was bad enough, but what Hood found more troubling was how to deal with his rookie deputy.

Hood summoned Young John, who entered his boss's office wearing a penitent, mortified expression Hood knew would make the task more difficult.

"How you feeling?" Hood asked.

"Better now."

"If you were feeling sick, why didn't you take a sick day?"

"Didn't think it was that bad. It was the smell in that apartment that got me."

Hood tented his fingers and leaned forward. "John, I need to level with you. We've got a problem here, and it's affecting your work. First, the accident with the cruiser, then you missed a shift, and I find you drunk, and now this."

"It's just . . . "

"I think you need to take a couple days and—" Hood began.

"I can't take off. I need to work. We need the money."

"We'll make it paid leave—three days. But I need you to see someone," Hood said. "The county has an EAP that allows you to see—"

"EAP? What's that?"

"Employee Assistance Program," Hood said. "You can see a mental health professional at no cost to you for the first six sessions."

"A shrink?"

"A counselor," Hood said. "Look, you said the other day you've been kind of overwhelmed lately."

"I'm not crazy," Young John said.

"That's not what I'm saying. This is non-negotiable, John. Your job performance has become more than erratic: it's downright dangerous. You saw how Cindy was shaking with that shotgun pointed at us. We were lucky this morning, and luck can run out fast in law enforcement."

Young John sat silently for a moment. "All right," he said, a whispered whimper.

Jacob Grace sat in the pristine examination room on the top floor of Doctors Park Medical Plaza, a three-story facility attached to Huhman County Hospital.

"Blood pressure is fine," said Dr. Daniels. He sat on a stool and tapped keys on a laptop computer. "Any pain today?"

Jacob pointed to the bandage concealing the wound where his ear had been severed. "Still hurts."

"How would you rate your pain?"

Jacob shrugged.

The doctor pointed to a scale depicting drawings ranging from a smiley face at 0 to a crying, frowny face at 10.

"I don't know. Five, maybe six. Doesn't a nurse usually do this stuff?" Jacob asked.

"She's busy." Daniels entered more data, arose from the stool, and moved to the examination table. "Hop up here," he said, patting the paper covering. "Let's have a look."

Jacob sat on the edge as Daniels removed the bandage. "Have you been keeping it clean?" the doctor asked.

"Best I can. Stayin' in a friend's stable, but it's got a sink and shower."

"Where's that?"

"Hutch's farm on Old Cedar Creek Road."

"Jesse Hutchschreider?"

"You know Hutch?" Jacob asked.

"Know the name. He boards horses, right?"

"My roommates. Noisy animals."

Daniels stepped back. "I don't see any signs of infection, but I'm going to give you something just to be safe."

After Jacob swallowed the medication, Daniels rebandaged the wound and instructed Jacob to see the receptionist to set up another appointment.

"Another appointment?"

"With something like this, you can't be too careful."

Jacob made the appointment and left the building. He crossed the lot to where Hutch had parked his pickup in a far corner. Hutch was sitting behind the wheel, blowing cigarette smoke through the open window when Jacob climbed into the passenger seat. "How'd it go?" Hutch asked.

"I don't think that doctor likes me."

"You're not really the warm, fuzzy type, Jacob."

"I don't think he trusts me, either."

Hutch tossed the cigarette out the window, started the ignition, and backed out of the parking space. "What makes you think so?"

"He wouldn't even let his nurse be in a closed room with me. He did everything himself—even took my blood pressure."

"Can't say I blame him." Hutch exited the lot.

"So, you don't trust me either. Guess that's why I'm

sleepin' in the stable."

"I haven't seen a change of heart in you, Jacob. I did some bad shit, too, but when I was in prison, I had a change of heart. I begged for His forgiveness and—"

"Why do I have to beg? Why can't God just forgive?" Jacob asked.

"He can. What you're talking about is grace—God's unmerited favor. I experience that now, but I never did until I accepted Jesus Christ as my Lord and Savior. That's when I dedicated myself to preaching His word during whatever time I have left here on Earth."

Jacob made no reply.

"You hear what I'm saying?" Hutch asked.

"I hear you. I'm just really tired right now."

In the nineteenth century, Father Josef Gottfried served as an evangelical Johnny Appleseed, planting Catholic churches throughout the Central Missouri area that would become Huhman County.

Father Gottfried's eye was on the eternal, not the temporal, but he lived long enough to see his work take root and grow. The ornate churches attracted German Catholic settlers, who gathered for worship, established businesses, built homes, and created communities connected by the railroads.

Time—and the gradual disappearance of rail service—eventually took its toll. Some communities surrendered to the death knell, but not all. Unwilling to abandon what they had built—including the magnificent stone churches with hand-carved altars bathed in the colorful illumination of stained-glass windows—some parishioners dug in their heels, relied on their work ethic, and trusted their faith. Ulrich, New Hermann, and Wessen were among the communities rejuvenated by micro-breweries, wineries and vineyards, resident artisans and craftsmen, and quaint bed and breakfast facilities that attracted tourists, created local jobs, and supported Catholic elementary schools.

Less fortunate was St. Bartholomew, a once-bustling community reduced to a death rattle. Many shops along its main street had succumbed to closure, their windows broken or shuttered. Two exceptions remained, Will's Market, located on the southeast corner, and St. Bartholomew Tavern, across the street and a few doors down.

Parked on a side street between the two businesses was an unmarked sheriff's department cruiser, where deputies Wally Wallendorf and Lester Stackhouse slumped in the front seat, trying to look inconspicuous while watching Will's Market. They were acting on information relayed by the prosecutor's office that drug suspect Joey Trammel had wasted no time seeking leniency by naming his supplier, Will Luebbering, the market's owner.

The officers waited and watched an elderly woman Wally recognized as Geneva Eckhart enter the store. Inactivity on the street resumed for nearly a half hour until a navy blue Olds Cutlass parked near the market. A young black man got out of the passenger side, and the car pulled away.

Wally and Lester both noted the car's license plate number was obscured. Neither recognized the passenger who had emerged.

"What do you think?" Lester asked.

"Let's stick with the kid," Wally answered.

The kid, Jet Johnson, stood in front of the market and looked up and down the street.

"Don't take this the wrong way," Wally said to his partner, "but have you ever known a black man to shop at Will's Market?"

"Don't recall seeing a black person anywhere in St. Bartholomew," Lester said. "Yours truly excluded, of course."

Jet pushed through one of the market's two glass-paned doors, sounding a bell positioned to signal that a customer had entered. The signal was unnecessary. A man standing behind the counter watched him warily with reddened, rheumy eyes.

Jet scanned the interior, pausing to glimpse into a convex mirror mounted high in a corner. The distorted reflection revealed a lone customer, an elderly woman standing in one of the half-dozen aisles and comparing prices on cans of corn. He turned to the counterman. "Looking for Will," he said.

"I'm Will." He stared at the unfamiliar customer. "And you are?"

"J.T. People call me Jet." He tilted his head toward the aisle, indicating suspicion about the elderly woman's presence.

"Don't worry about her," Will said. "She can't hear shit."

"My friend Randy said he was gonna call you. Set things up."

"Yeah, he called. So how do you know Randy?"

"Met in St. Louis."

"Tell me about him."

"Like what?"

Will shrugged. "Like, anything."

Jet looked at the aisle openings, then back at Will. "What's this about, man? Randy said this would be cool."

"Just want to make sure it stays cool."

"He wears a mitten on his right hand. It ain't normal. That what you wanna know?"

Will looked in the convex mirror and saw that Geneva Eckhart had advanced one aisle. "You know," he said, focusing on the mirror but addressing Jet, "this is the shit I have to deal with. She comes in here every three days, shops for nearly an hour, and always buys the same half dozen items." He faced Jet. "You go out the front, walk around back to the loading dock, and wait. I'll be there as soon as she's done. Should be about five, ten minutes."

Jet did as instructed. He lingered behind the store in its gravel parking area, bordered by a split-rail fence entangled in weeds and vines. Beyond was an unmown backyard littered with a dismembered vehicle, a rusted barbecue grill, and a weathered washing machine. When Jet heard the sound of the overhead garage door opening, he jumped onto the loading dock and faced Will.

"Ready to do some business?" Will asked. Jet nodded and followed him into the rear storeroom, where shelves lining the walls displayed cans, bottles, boxes, and cardboard cartons were stacked on wooden pallets in the center of the concrete floor.

"Need to see some money, man," Will said. He pulled the overhead door closed. "What're you in the market for? Got a new batch of meth made right here in Mid-Mo."

"Randy said you got some grade-A crack." Jet removed a wad of bills from his pants pocket and slapped it on top of a cardboard carton.

"Can do," Will said. He removed a Cap'n Crunch cereal box from an upper shelf and set it beside the cash. He was opening the lid when the bell in the store chimed, signaling someone had entered. "Fuck," Will said. "Should've closed up early. Stay here, stay quiet."

Will opened the door slightly and saw a uniformed deputy approaching hurriedly. "Deputy," Will said as he blocked the half-open door to the storage area.

Jet grabbed for his cash, but it fell between two cardboard cartons. He panicked and flung open the rear overhead door, only to find a second uniformed deputy on the loading dock. Jet faked left and sprinted right. The deputy reached but failed to grasp Jet before he jumped from the dock. Jet momentarily lost his balance in the gravel but regained it and came up running.

"I got him," Lester shouted. He turned, leaped from the dock, and hurried in pursuit.

Jet hurdled the fence and, like a broken-field running back, dodged obstacles, tipping over a barbecue grill into Lester's path.

Lester, a college athlete whose pro prospects were ended by a knee injury, initially lost some ground but was able to keep the suspect in sight as they bisected a residential neighborhood that yielded to an open field ascending the hill toward St. Bartholomew's.

Winded by the time he approached the rear of the church, Jet glanced behind and saw the persistent deputy beginning to narrow the gap between them. Jet scurried around the building, pulled a handgun from his jacket pocket and, while still running, looked back and fired in a desperate attempt to slow or stop his pursuer.

The bullet ricocheted off the sidewalk and caught Lester in the shin. He shouted in pain and went down.

As Lester watched the suspect hurdle a short, stone wall and disappear from view, he grimaced and grabbed his lower leg in a vain effort to lessen what felt like an agonizing electric shock radiating from his nerve endings.

He activated the radio on his shoulder, triggering a buzz of static. "Wally."

"Yeah," came the chief deputy's voice. "You get him?"

"No," Lester answered.

"Where are you? You don't sound good."

"I'm not," Lester said. "Son of a bitch shot me."

CHAPTER
10

Hood was awakened from fitful sleep by the ring tone of his cell phone, which he kept on his bedside nightstand. He lifted himself onto an elbow and looked at the illuminated screen that displayed the time, 2:45 a.m., and the caller, the dispatcher.

"Hood," he answered.

"Sorry to bother you," Amber said, "but I thought you'd want to hear this right away. I just dispatched a deputy and an ambulance to Jesse Hutchschreider's farm in response to a call from him. He said Jacob Grace has been attacked—again."

"Hutch's farm?"

"Yes, the address is—"

"I know it," Hood said. "On my way."

He dressed quickly and sped to the scene, passing both the Jobe and Grace farms on Route AA before turning north onto Old Cedar Creek Road and into Jesse Hutchschreider's driveway. The scene was awash in light. The strobes atop the cruiser and ambulance pulsed red-blue rhythms amid the bright outdoor floodlights. Interior lights were visible through the windows and screen door. One of Hood's deputies, Arthur

Koeningsfeld, stood on the large porch.

"What've we got, Art?" Hood asked as he approached.

"Somebody cut off Jacob's nose."

"His nose?" Hood said, incredulous.

"Well, part of it, at least."

"Details?"

"Haven't talked to him yet. EMTs told me to be patient. Figured I'd wait out here."

Hood motioned for Art to follow him and, together, they entered the house and traced the sound of voices to a spacious kitchen, where Jacob Grace was lying on his back on a kitchen table. As they entered, an EMT Hood knew only as Mike left the room while a second attendant Hood didn't recognize applied a wad of sterile gauze to Jacob's wound.

Standing alone at the kitchen counter was Hutch. His facial scars, shaved head, and tattooed arms reminded Hood more of the ex-con he was than the preacher he had become. In his younger days, Hutch was a self-described "hell-raiser," a pursuit that ended with a five-year prison term for aggravated assault. He was reborn in a cell and—after his release—began preaching the Gospel as pastor of Friendship Church in rural Huhman County.

"Can anybody tell me what happened?" Hood asked.

"The tip of this man's nose has been severed," the EMT answered.

"With what?" Hood asked.

"Looks like some kind of pruning shears or limb lopper."

"Who did it?" Hood persisted. "Anybody see anything?"

Jacob shook his head slightly, indicating no, which prompted the EMT to say, "Stay still. Let me get this bleeding under control."

"Hutch?" Hood asked.

"All I know is the screaming woke me up. I looked out the window and saw Jacob running up the hill from the stable where he's staying. I came downstairs, brought him in here, and called for help."

"See anyone else?"

"Nope," Hutch said.

The EMT, apparently satisfied the bleeding had been stanched, began bandaging Jacob's nose. "Okay, Mr. Grace," he said. "We're going to get you to a hospital, see if they can get that nose reattached."

"Find it?" Hood said, surprised.

"My partner's looking for it now."

Hood, fearing contamination of the crime scene, left the kitchen, followed by Art. Together, they hurried along the gravel drive that sloped downhill to the stable, which remained dark.

As they approached, Mike exited the sliding door in the center. "No lights," he said. "I felt around and finally found the switch, but nothing happened. Something must have tripped the breaker."

"Or someone," Hood said. He had forgotten his flashlight, but Art produced a department-issue model attached to his belt. "Let's have a look."

They stepped inside the stable, and Art swept the

flashlight beam across the interior. A horse whinnied, triggering a cacophony of equine sounds.

"Breaker box," Mike announced when the light source illuminated it.

Hood walked to the power source, removed a handkerchief, and used it to cover his fingertip as he flipped the main. Light flooded the interior, revealing rows of horse stalls on both sides and two small rooms in opposite corners.

The men approached the nearest room and peeked through the open doorway at the arrangement of saddles, bridles, and other tack. They walked the length of the wide center aisle to the second enclosure, outfitted as a spartan bedroom.

"Wait out here," Hood instructed. He took the flashlight from Art and stepped across the threshold into the room.

"Remember," Mike reminded, "I need that nose."

Hood scrutinized the interior. The walls and floors were unadorned wooden planks. A worn canvas duffel bag rested on a lone, rickety wooden chair. The single bed was partially covered by a plaid blanket. The bed sheet and pillow were stained with blood, presumably Jacob's.

Hood inspected the bed, blanket, and pillow. No nose. He got on his hands and knees and looked under the bed and chair. Again, nothing.

"I'm gonna need to get the crime lab out here," he said to Art, who stood outside the room.

Mike raised himself on his toes and peered over Art's shoulder. "What about the nose?"

Hood shook his head. "No nose."

The man in the hospital bed looked like an inverse Frankenstein creation—instead of body parts stitched together, facial features were missing.

Where the tip of his nose had been, Jacob Grace wore a bandage similar to the one covering the wound where his left ear had been.

"What do you want?" he asked his visitor, the sheriff.

"I'm here for your statement," Hood said. He stood at the bedside, a notebook in his left hand and a pen in his right.

"Didn't see nothin'."

"That's not a statement. What time did you go to bed?"

"Early. Maybe nine. I was dog-tired. Hutch took me to my doctor's appointment in the morning, then had me run a big pile of brush through his wood chipper all afternoon. We had some stew. I went down to my room, had me a few drinks, and went to bed."

"A few drinks?"

"No more than normal. I didn't pass out or nothin'. Just went to sleep. I was sleeping pretty good, too, until I felt this sharp pain, grabbed my face, and felt blood. I jumped out of bed and flicked the light switch—nothin'—so I groped my way to the door and ran up to the house, screamin' and shoutin' for Hutch."

"Did you see anyone?"

"Nope."

"Did Hutch answer the door right away?" Hood asked, contemplating whether to add the homeowner to his suspect list.

"Took a minute or two. I was poundin' on it."

"And you didn't see anyone else?"

"No."

Hood asked, speaking slowly and emphatically, "Do you have any idea who did this?"

"No."

Hood glanced at the blank notebook page, a testament to his lack of progress. In both attacks, the assailant remained unseen, left no identifying clues, and took whatever weapon was used along with the severed body parts.

"Jacob, I'm trying to solve this case," Hood said, his frustration apparent. "It's not because—"

Jacob formed a thin smile. "Must be a bitch."

"What?"

"Helpin' me. Must be a bitch; you bein' sheriff and me bein' a killer and all."

"I took an oath," Hood said. "It's my job."

Jacob shrugged. "So do it."

"I'm trying, but it would help if you gave me something to go on."

"I told you. I don't know nothin'."

Hood looked into Jacob's eyes. He recalled Clarence Jobe's description of Jacob as a "hard man," as well as the three-decades old trial transcripts depicting Jacob as uncooperative in his defense and unapologetic about the murders. What, Hood wondered, could possess a man to kill his own wife and children? When Jacob met his gaze, Hood said, "Did you ever say why you did what you did all those years ago? Did you ever confess or apologize—even to your Maker?"

"Fuck you," Jacob spat.

"Do you even know why?"

"Get the fuck outta my room."

In that moment, Hood suspected he might never learn the answer. Jacob, he believed, would carry his thirty-year secret to his grave. He got the fuck out of Jacob's room.

Angela sat at her oak kitchen table opposite Randy, the childhood friend she had reconnected with at her fundraiser. Prince—her ever-present canine companion—positioned himself beside Angela, between his owner and her guest. He focused on Randy, who gnawed his trademark toothpick and drank black coffee while Angela sipped chamomile tea through a straw which she slipped beneath her navy blue veil.

"I'm glad you called," she said. "I was hoping you would, but I wasn't sure."

Randy shrugged slightly. "You're one of the few good things I remember about this town."

"So what have you been up to for the last—what—twenty-some years?"

"Mom dragged me around for a while. I mostly grew up in Florida after we moved in with Aunt Esther, my mom's sister. She was a bigger religious fanatic than Mom. It was all 'God this, God that. God will provide.' It was hell. Home sucked; school sucked." Randy looked at his mittened hand. "I got picked on, bullied, just like here. I got into trouble, but you don't want to hear that."

Angela leaned forward. "It's okay to talk about it. I remember what it was like for us—being different. It was hard."

"Yeah, well it didn't get easier," Randy said. "After Aunt Esther died—Mom said God 'called her home,' but I think He just got pissed—we moved around again for a while. Finally, we moved to St. Louis so Mom could take care of a cousin who was dying of cancer. After he passed away, we stayed there for a while. Then Mom suffered a bad stroke around Christmas and died in February."

"I'm sorry to hear that."

"Don't be. It was a blessing. She was in bad shape."

"And you took care of her?"

Randy looked beyond the kitchen window at some distant point. "Yeah. Best I could."

"Did your father help?"

Randy snorted a derisive laugh.

"He could at least have given you money to care for her," Angela said. "Did you call him?"

"I don't ask him for anything."

The resentment in his tone cued Angela to drop the subject. "Must have been hard—working and being her caregiver."

Randy refocused on his mitten. "I get disability," he whispered. He looked up at her. "And you," he said, brightening at the prospect of a new topic. "What's been going on in your life?"

"Well, after my guardians moved me from public to private school, my teachers saw how I excelled at art. They encouraged me, and I was able to get a scholarship—"

She stopped in mid-sentence when Odessa appeared in the kitchen doorway. "Sorry to interrupt," Odessa said, "but Ethan is here. Says he has some papers you need to sign."

"Yes." Angela turned to Randy. "I'm sorry, but I do need to sign these. Do you mind?"

"No."

Angela instructed Odessa to bring Ethan to the kitchen where she introduced him to Randy, invited him to sit at the table, and offered him coffee or tea, which he declined.

Prince stood while the two men shook hands, prompting Angela to lean toward the dog and whisper assurance. Nevertheless, Ethan moved to a seat opposite Prince before placing a pen and stack of documents on the table and sliding them across.

"Please," Angela invited her guests. "Feel free to get to know each other while I sign these."

Their exchange was more an interrogation of Randy than a conversation, and Angela felt relieved when she heard a knock at the front door. She looked at the wall clock and guessed the newest visitor was the sheriff, who had called earlier and made an appointment. Her assumption was confirmed moments later when Odessa escorted him into the kitchen.

"Hello, Sheriff," Angela greeted. "You've met Ethan. And this is Randy Da—oops, I forgot—Knaebel. He's a friend from childhood."

"Nice to meet you," Hood said.

"Likewise."

Both Randy and Ethan arose and offered handshakes, again alerting Prince to readiness. During the process, Hood noticed Randy's right hand was covered with a mitten.

"May I?" Hood asked, gesturing to the empty chair near Prince and Angela.

"Of course," Angela said.

"I mean, may I pet Prince?" Hood clarified as he sat.

"Certainly." She spoke a command; the shepherd sat, his posture relaxed.

"The sheriff and I have an appointment," Angela announced while Hood petted Prince and patted his flank. "Randy and I were just catching up," she continued, as if Hood deserved an explanation. "We haven't seen each other since we were kids. And Ethan popped in to get me to sign some papers." She signed the final document, straightened the stack, and put down the pen.

Hood looked upward at Randy and Ethan, who had remained standing, facing each other in a silent stalemate. "So," Angela said to them, "if you'll excuse us, the sheriff and I have a matter to discuss."

Hood sensed an almost palpable tension between the two men. Each appeared irritated by the presence of the other. He couldn't decide if Ethan's unmistakable expression of disdain was directed at Randy's crude toothpick habit or at the man himself.

Angela waited until Odessa escorted the two men out,

then said to Hood, "I'm afraid the coffee's gone. I can brew more unless you'd like some tea."

Hood wasn't much of a tea drinker, but Angela had extended an unexpected courtesy by inviting him to her kitchen, and he didn't want to seem ungracious. "Tea is fine."

"It's chamomile," she said. With Prince shadowing her movements, she retrieved a cup and saucer from a cabinet, poured, and placed the cup in front of him.

"Thank you."

When she and Prince were settled, Hood said, "I'm here again with news about your father."

"I'm listening."

"He was assaulted again. This time someone cut off the tip of his nose."

"His nose?"

"Yes."

"Very well," she said and pushed back her chair in preparation to stand.

"I need your help."

"My help?"

"Yes."

"With what, exactly?"

Hood wasn't sure. He was delighted she was still sitting, still willing at least to hear him out. The investigation was about determining who was systematically mutilating Jacob Grace, but Hood suspected there was more to it. Hood knew his customary method—organize, classify, tie up loose ends, follow clues—wasn't working. And he couldn't deny his uneasy feeling that some indefinable something was at work.

After a long pause, he answered, "Resolution."

"Regarding the attacks on my father?"

"I think they're connected to an event in the past. I believe—"

"You don't need to try to spare my feelings, Sheriff," Angela said. "You can say murders or massacre. After all, I was there."

"Okay," Hood said, bolstered by her fortitude. "Do you have any idea why your father killed your family members?"

"None."

"Do you know if he ever told anyone?"

"Did you read the trial transcript?"

"No, but I read the docket entries and the case summary."

"I have no idea. Maybe you should ask him."

"I did," Hood said. "At the hospital. Just before I came here."

"What did he say?"

"He told me to get out, expletive deleted."

They sat quietly at the table.

Angela bent her head and sipped tea through her straw.

Hood thought about his recovery program's recommendation to assess his own motives, attitudes, and behaviors. "I couldn't live with myself after doing something like that." Hood's whispered words were barely audible, as if thinking aloud. "I just don't understand."

"I had to stop trying—to understand, I mean. It became an obsession. Was there anything I could have done to prevent it? Was this God's Will? Why would God allow something like this? It shattered what little faith I had. Call me whatever—atheist, agnostic. Those are just words, hollow labels. How do I believe in a God, let alone love or have faith in, a God who would let that happen?"

Hood shrugged slightly.

"The only way I could come to terms with this," Angela said, "was to tell myself maybe this wasn't for me—for any of us, for that matter—to understand. Maybe my father doesn't even understand why he did what he did."

The sheriff silently shook his head. He wasn't convinced.

CHAPTER

11

Wally peered through the open doorway of his boss's office.
"Any word on Lester?" he asked, concerned about his fellow deputy's gunshot wound.

"Says he's fine," Hood answered. "Bullet took a chunk of flesh, but it was mostly a graze. He's on crutches, but he's already walking around."

"He hates being sidelined," Wally said.

"I told him to take some time off. He's got plenty of sick days."

"Well, don't be surprised if he hobbles into work."

Hood considered the comment. The absences—first Young John, now Lester—were beginning to take a toll. Workloads among remaining staff were increasing, and investigations were languishing.

"Anything new on the Jacob Grace assaults?" Wally asked.

Hood shook his head. The investigation had stalled—not for lack of attention, but for lack of evidence.

"That bad, huh?" Wally remarked.

"Got a few minutes?" Hood asked. He knew from

experience that talking through a case with another deputy could provide a new perspective. And Wally's insights had been particularly helpful in the past.

"Sure," Wally said. He entered the office and sat.

"For starters," Hood said, "I've got too many suspects and none of them stand out."

"Run through them for me."

"Well, there's Jacob's daughter, Angela. On paper, as the lone survivor of the massacre, she's the prime suspect. She's hard to figure out. She's still got scars, both physical and emotional. She's intelligent, somewhat disarming. When I first met her, she was kind of cold and detached—I couldn't decide if she was being defensive or if it was just an act. But since that first meeting, she's warmed up some.

"There's also some people who are very close to her. One is Odessa, her live-in assistant. She was an orphan, and Angela took her in. She's very protective of Angela. Another is Angela's lawyer, Ethan Diffenbaugh. Know him?"

Wally shook his head.

"Me neither. I met with him the other day. He does contract law, not criminal cases. Kind of pompous. I get a feeling he has a thing for Angela, but his interest may just be her money. It'd be nice to know how much he depends on her to maintain his high-end lifestyle."

"That it?" Wally said.

"I wish," Hood said. "There's some other people on the fringes. I wouldn't mention their names except I know it'll stay right here. Jesse Hutchschreider is letting Jacob stay in his stables. Maybe Hutch really is into helping others these days, but it sure makes it easy for him to keep an eye on Jacob's whereabouts. And Clarence Jobe was the neighbor who was with Jacob's wife when she died on the front porch. He still rents and farms some of Angela's acreage. And Jacob's wife was a Bunch, sister of Andrew Bunch, who also happens to be Young John's father."

When Wally made no response, Hood added, "That's it."

"Alibis?"

"No good ones, but the assaults happened in the middle of the night, so it's hard to disprove when people say they were asleep."

"Motives?"

"Nothing solid. Everyone sees Angela as the victim and Jacob as the villain. I can't help thinking someone is trying to avenge Angela's loss. The scenario fits with the missing body parts."

"The proverbial avenging angel," Wally said.

Hood nodded in the same instant Maggie appeared in the doorframe.

"Sorry to butt in," she said, addressing Hood, "but Andrew Bunch is here. He insists on seeing you. He's pretty steamed. I also think he's had a few."

"I'd better talk to him."

Maggie left.

"Want me to stay?" Wally asked.

"Probably better if I see him alone."

"Okay. But I'll be next door if you need me."

"Thanks," Hood said. "And thanks for listening."

"Sure."

As Wally exited, Hood stood, moved to the doorway, and watched Andrew approach.

An animator might draw Andrew as a banty rooster, a small, freckle-faced, combustible redhead. He seemed always on the defensive, quick to construe any gesture or remark as a personal putdown. Hood often wondered how Andrew balanced his hair-trigger temper with his customer service duties as manager of Bunch Farm and Home.

Although Hood sat and offered his visitor a seat, Andrew declined. "This won't take long," Andrew said. He closed the office door.

The action rankled Hood, but he realized almost immediately he was reflecting Andrew's aggravation. "What can I do for you?" he asked.

"My son doesn't have a problem. I just want you to know that."

"I never said he did."

"He told me you put him on leave to see a doctor."

"I did," Hood affirmed.

"There's nothing wrong with him. He ain't sick."

Hood stood. He preferred talking with people at eye level. "This is a personnel matter, Andrew," he said. "It's confidential. What your son chooses to tell you is his business, but I won't discuss it."

"Why not?"

"Because it isn't appropriate."

"You sayin' you can't tell me what's going on?"

"That's exactly what I'm saying."

"You think he's been drinkin' too much, don't you?"

"Again, it's not appropriate for me to—"

"Because men drink. I've seen you hoist a beer or two at parish picnics. I drink. My son drinks. It's what men do. So what?"

Before recovery, Hood did drink—at home, at restaurants, at parish picnics, and other community events. Because of his job—an elected, high-profile law enforcement position—he purposely avoided public intoxication. He would drink a beer or two in public, then adjourn to the privacy of his home to continue. Eventually, his drinking escalated to the point where he was unable to stop until he passed out or blacked out.

"Andrew," Hood said, his tone authoritative. "You're a friend and John's father, so I'm going to tell you this much. Your son is an excellent deputy, but his performance has been inconsistent lately. This is not a punishment. I did what I think is in his best interest."

Andrew stared at the sheriff. "I don't buy it."

"Well, it's the truth."

"So that's it?"

"That's it," Hood said, with unmistakable finality.

Andrew opened the door and left.

"You fucking did what?" Randy's voice exploded.

"I didn't mean to," Jet said. "It just happened."

"You just happened to shoot a cop?"

"I was with that Will's Market guy you set me up with. We got busted, man. I took off runnin', but one cop chased me. I couldn't lose 'im. I ran a long way but, when I looked back, he was still comin'. I was just tryin' to get 'im to stop."

"So that's why you called and told me not to pick you up."

"Look, I didn't mean to hit the guy."

"It doesn't fucking matter what you meant," Randy said. "You know what kind of shit storm this'll bring."

Jet hesitated. "Okay, I fucked up. What are we gonna do?"

"We?"

The monosyllable hit Jet like a gut punch. "Yeah, we. We're partners."

"And sometimes partners need to split up."

Jet stared, his expression a mixture of disbelief and anger.

"At least for a while," Randy added, softening his tone. "Maybe you should go back to St. Louis and lay low."

Jet shook his head. "There's a shit storm waiting for me there, too. The Street Kings have long memories."

"Well, you're going to have to get invisible if you stick around here."

"Okay," Jet said, his voice contrite. "We do one more job and—"

Randy smacked his forehead with an open palm. "Are you fucking kidding me? Every cop in Central Missouri is looking for you right now. This is no time to do a job."

"I got no cash and no product, man. I'm tapped."

"Count yourself lucky. You could be in a cell looking at serious time," Randy said, his exasperation apparent. "Look, we'll find you a hidey hole and I'll do what I can." He tapped his head with a forefinger. "But you need to think about staying put."

"So, how are the illustrations coming along?" Ethan asked.

Angela knew he was referring to her progress on the children's book illustrating the major religions. "Okay," she said. She turned her attention from Ethan—who sat across from her at her kitchen table—and looked through a window. The sky was a shade darker than gun-metal grey, and a persistent rain pattered a steady rhythm on the roof. "I'm working on the section depicting Christianity."

"I would think that would be the easiest one."

It hadn't been, but she didn't correct him. She only nodded.

"Good," he said. "We've got deadlines."

His use of the pronoun "we" disturbed her. She stared at him but said nothing.

"Are you hiding your trademark sharp objects in the drawings?"

"Illustrations," she corrected.

"Illustrations," he repeated. "Because the publisher seemed to want them. At least, that's the impression I got."

"Of course he wants them. It'll sell more books," she said, a hint of derision in her tone.

"So you'll include them?"

"We'll see if he can find them."

Ethan leaned back in his chair and sighed dramatically. "Are you okay?"

"Yes. Why?"

"You seem distracted."

"I'm fine," she lied.

"Because, you know, these attacks on your father and the appearance of this Randy guy . . . " He left the thought unfinished.

"What about Randy?"

Ethan spread his hands. "He just turns up—all of a sudden, like. Just seems strange, that's all."

Angela pondered the possibilities. She had sensed tension between Ethan and Randy. Was Ethan jealous? Did he see Randy as a rival? She knew Ethan felt some bizarre attraction to her, which she had dismissed largely as sexual curiosity. "Randy's an old friend. He's back in town," Angela said. "That's all."

"That's not all."

Angela thought he sounded smug. "What do you mean?"

"He's got a record, a criminal record, misdemeanor trespassing and felony stealing."

"You did a background check on him?" she asked, incredulous.

"It's public record. Anyone can do it. I just ran his name through case.net, and the crimes popped up."

Angela looked away. "I can't believe it."

Ethan leaned forward and folded his hands on the tabletop. "I'm just trying to protect you."

"I don't need protection."

"Well, inform you, then. It never hurts to be informed."

They sat silently for a time before Angela said, "I'd better get back to work. I've got—I'm sorry, we've got—those deadlines, you know."

Hood was furious. He lingered outside the door of the interrogation room, willing his anger to subside before entering. He recalled Matthew telling him anger was a secondary emotion caused by something else—humiliation, hurt feelings, even fears. He decided that wasn't true in this case; he was pissed because someone had shot one of his deputies.

He thought about the two people on the other side of the door.

William "Will" Luebbering III was no stranger to the St. Bartholomew community or Huhman County law enforcement. He had become the sole proprietor of the family market handed down through generations but also had descended into drug addiction and dealing. Will previously had served shock detention in the Huhman County Jail and a probationary term for possession of a controlled substance.

With him would be Bernie Thompson, an experienced attorney who had counseled Will's father and grandfather on business matters and, more recently, had revived his criminal practice to defend Will. Hood suspected the attorney would prefer a reasonable deal instead of the vagaries of a trial.

RICHARD F. MCGONEGAL

He entered the spartan room designed for a singular function. The walls were bare, with the exception of a large, rectangular, one-way glass that allowed observation from an adjoining room. A corner-mounted camera focused on Will and Bernie, who already were seated at a wooden table, leaving two empty chairs.

Hood stared for a long moment at Will, then said, without preamble, "I only want to know one thing: who shot my deputy?"

"My client doesn't know the man," Bernie answered. "He's never seen him before."

Hood remained focused on Will, ignoring the lawyer. "Will, I know you. You're not careless. You wouldn't sell drugs to—"

"Whoa," Bernie interrupted. "My client doesn't acknowledge any illegal drug transaction. A stranger entered my client's market—"

"Stop," Hood commanded. "The camera's not running and there's nobody behind the glass. My interest in a pissant drug deal is nothing compared to who shot my deputy."

"My client isn't prepared at this time—"

"Stop," Hood repeated. "I'm not in the mood. We all know how this works. Will doesn't want to give me a name because it's bad for business, scares off the customers. But there's two ways this can go. I get a name, I tell the prosecutor you cooperated, and I move on to other things. I don't get a name, I've got two deputies who witnessed two men in a storage room where cash and drugs were confiscated."

Will and Bernie looked at each other for a long moment before Will said to the sheriff, "Give us a second."

After Hood left the room, Will whispered to his attorney, "Thing is, I know this kid only as J.T. or Jet. He's nothing to me, but I'm no rat."

"My inclination is to wait," Bernie advised. "Hood's pushing hard. He's upset about his deputy—that's part of it—but he also may realize the case is weak. From what you've told me, the deputies didn't witness any deal or transaction. Hood didn't even use the word. The cash and the drugs were just there in the storeroom. Nobody was holding them. I can create all kinds of reasonable doubt, particularly if they don't find this Jet guy. Who's to say he didn't bring the drugs to your market?"

Will nodded.

"Plus," Bernie continued. "We don't even know what kind of charges Hood will seek or what the prosecutor will file. Admittedly, if they find this Jet, we lose a bargaining chip, but I think our best bet is to wait and see."

"Okay."

Bernie arose, walked to the door and rapped on it.

When Hood opened it, Bernie said, "Sorry to disappoint you, Sheriff, but we have nothing more to say at this time."

"I'm going to find this guy," Hood said, "with or without your help."

CHAPTER

12

"This next race could be called 'running from the law,'" the announcer said, drawing a mixture of groans and laughter from the crowd. "That's Sheriff Francis Hood in lane two with Doxie and, at the other end, Doxie's owner, Chief Deputy Wally Wallendorf."

Hood tipped his hat to the spectators pressed against the orange snow fence separating them from the grassy rectangle designated as the racecourse. He wasn't entirely sure how Wally had talked him into participating. The occasion was the annual Octoberfest, a festival spanning two blocks—the entire downtown—of New Gottfried. Among the featured events were the Dachshund Derby races. Wally regularly entered his beloved canine in the annual event, which she invariably failed to finish.

Wally had pleaded with his boss: "All you need to do is let her go when they give the signal." The deputy had planned for his oldest son to assist, but none of his three boys had returned from scouting for funnel cakes by the time Doxie's qualifying heat was announced.

"I'm in uniform. I'm on duty," Hood had said.

"It'll take two minutes."

Hood had relented and found himself among a foursome squatting or kneeling at the chalked starting line. The common denominator among the diverse group—a county sheriff, a gangly teenager, a septuagenarian, and a young girl—was that each restrained an excited dachshund.

"Ready," the announcer called.

Doxie squirmed free of Hood's grasp. "No," he shouted.

The announcer failed to hear him amid the escalating crowd noise, but it didn't matter. Doxie didn't run away; she rolled onto her back, inviting a tummy rub.

"Set," the announcer said as Hood scooped up the pooch and repositioned her.

"Go."

Hood released the wiener dog, and Doxie dashed away, but not to Wally, who frantically called her name and waved his arms. Instead, Doxie veered to the snow fence bordering the right side and poked her nose through the orange mesh where a previous racer was being rewarded with a doggie biscuit.

The race ended within seconds, and Hood and Wally gathered where Doxie stood at the sideline, wagging her tail and begging for a handout.

"Another humiliating defeat," Wally joked as he lifted the dog into his arms. "Well, you know what they say— there's always next year."

Hood patted his deputy's shoulder, straightened into his

sheriff's posture, and resumed his patrol of the festival grounds. He walked along the center of the blocked street, where members of the Central Missouri Old Car Club had angle-parked their vintage vehicles. The restored automobiles ranged from model T's and model A's to Nash Ramblers and AMC Javelins; from immaculate T-Birds and Mustangs to 1970s muscle cars, including a 426 Hemi 'Cuda and a 454 Chevelle SS.

The collection warmed Hood with nostalgia and appreciation for the people who preserved and reconditioned these remnants of a mechanical age predating the advent of digital technology.

The steeple bell at Annunciation Catholic Church tolled 2 p.m. as Hood approached the facade and spotted Linda, who, as always, was punctual. His wife watched him with the familiar bemused, fascinated expression that always caused him to wonder what she was thinking.

"Hi," he greeted.

"You're right on time."

They kissed—the casual, easy kiss of long-time partners.

"Hungry?" Hood asked.

"Starved. I usually eat earlier."

"You should have said something. I could have—"

"This is fine," she said. "I'm just glad you suggested it."

They walked arm in arm, following the signs to the church's side entrance, which led to the basement cafeteria.

"I can't decide whether to get brats or pot roast," Hood said as they joined the line.

"I'm going with the German pot roast." Linda lifted two

plastic trays and passed one to her husband. "Been thinking about it all morning."

"Talked me into it."

After getting their dinners and sitting beside each other, Hood settled into the warm ambiance, delicious meal, and comfortable conversations of intimates catching up on each other's life. The sensation reminded him of how much he missed these moments and prompted the discouraging realization this one would end with each going a separate way. "So how are things in the Kampeter household?"

Linda used her fork to cut the tender roast. "Okay, but I worry about wearing out our welcome."

"How so?"

"Oh, it's not anything they've said or done. Actually, they've both been very gracious." She took a delicate bite, chewed, and swallowed. "But I can't help but feel we're an imposition. It's been like two months now."

Hood was tempted to say, "More like nine weeks," but didn't. Instead, he said, "You and Elizabeth can come home any time. You know that."

She placed her fork on the table, then reached out and covered his left hand. "I know, Francis, and I appreciate that. It's just, I'm not ready yet."

He nodded to signal he understood, although he didn't entirely.

She tightened her grip on his hand. "I'm supportive of what you're doing. I'm not staying away to punish you. I hope you know that. But I have to heal, too."

Hood looked at his plate, where a few morsels remained. "I guess I'm still making this about me."

"You're doing great," she encouraged. "Sarah says recovery is a process. It takes time."

"Some people in the program talk about an alcoholic having two personalities, the addicted self and the real self. I was like that—the sober, responsible sheriff and the late-night guy who couldn't stop drinking once he started. Then that guy started taking over the other guy's life."

Linda squeezed his hand. "And now that you've stopped drinking, you're not indulging that alcoholic self."

"I'm trying to kill him is what I'm doing, but it's a slow, painful death. I think what I may be experiencing on some level is grief."

"Do you think you need to see a professional counselor?" Linda whispered. "I mean, what you said makes sense. Sarah says giving up alcohol was like losing a faithful friend who was always there for her."

"I'll think about it. I will. I really will. Sometimes it's just tough." He was tempted to add, "particularly when I'm alone," but didn't.

"You're making progress." Then, as if Linda had read his thoughts, she added, "It's just that if I came home now and you started drinking again, I don't think I could bear it."

Hood stared at his empty plate. "I know. I kept telling myself I wasn't hurting anyone else—particularly you or Elizabeth—to justify my drinking. I was in such denial. I didn't see it then, but I do now."

"And," Linda replied, "I had to start putting up walls to protect myself. It's going to take time for them to come down."

Hood wondered if they ever would come down. Matthew had been blunt: once an alcoholic, always an alcoholic. The disease could be arrested, but not cured. Could he trust himself not to drink again? Could he expect Linda and Elizabeth ever to trust him again?

"Oh," Linda said, glancing at the wall clock. "I need to get going. I signed up for the next shift at the auxiliary's bake sale."

Hood and Linda walked together, exchanging greetings with friends and acquaintances they met along the way. A festival atmosphere prevailed, and Hood felt his uniformed presence as a law enforcement officer was unnecessary. People shopped and conversed under the colorful canopies and awnings advertising everything from custom jewelry to custard, from water softeners to waffle fries.

He left Linda at her booth and wandered to the beer garden—an array of tables and chairs shaded by a massive canopy tent with canvas roof flaps promoting its sponsor, Raithel Bros. Insurance. Across a closed side street was a flatbed trailer where the country band Southern Cross performed. On the street's asphalt surface, a smattering of people were line dancing.

Hood stepped into the welcome shade provided by the beer garden's canopy and spotted Jesse Hutchschreider seated at a table conversing with a man Hood didn't know.

"Hello, Hutch," Hood said. "How's the patient?" he added, referencing Jacob Grace.

"Damned ugly, if you ask me."

"Heard you gave him a place to stay," Hutch's companion said. "I wouldn't give him the time of day after what he done."

Hood extended his hand to the man. "I'm your sheriff, Francis Hood."

"Billy Van Loo," the man said, clasping Hood's hand. "We met, but it was some time ago. You were running for office, as I recollect."

Hood nodded in recognition, connecting Billy's name to a corn and soybean farm near the county's eastern border. "Good to see you," Hood said. "You know Jacob well?"

"Hell no. Thought he was still doin' time 'til I heard Hutch was helping him."

The conversation was interrupted by Clarence Jobe, who was carrying a full pitcher of beer to his table, but stopped to greet Hood. "Afternoon, Sheriff," Clarence said, touching the bill of his cap. He looked at the men seated at the table and added, "Hutch, Billy."

Hood sensed—from the tone and exchange of icy looks—that the relationship between Clarence and the other farmers was, if not hostile, certainly strained.

"Come join us at our table," Clarence invited the sheriff. "Mary Agnes is there and some of her folks. We got a fresh pitcher and plenty of cups."

"Thanks," Hood said. "I'll come sit for a minute, but I'll pass on the beer."

"On duty, huh? I get it." Clarence pointed to a far table. "Well, we're right over there."

Hood exchanged good-byes with Hutch and Billy, then joined the Jobes at their table. The conversation touched on various topics, including rainfall, the recent harvest, and commodity prices. Hood mostly listened and was about ready to excuse himself when Andrew Bunch approached.

"Can't believe you fired my boy," he said to Hood. Andrew held a nearly full cup of beer, and his speech was slurred enough to indicate he already was intoxicated.

"I didn't fire him," Hood said. "He's on leave."

"'Cause you botched a drug bust at the projects," Andrew spat. His face was reddened and his tone combative.

"I have no intention of discussing—"

"Coverin' your own ass is what I think."

"Andrew, this is not the time or the place," Hood warned. His cell phone rang and identified the caller as Lester. "I need to take this," he said to Andrew, then stepped away and answered the call.

"He's here," Lester said. "The kid who shot me."

"You walkin' away from me?" Andrew shouted.

"Where are you?" Hood asked Lester.

"Annunciation Church cafeteria," his deputy answered. "Me and my wife are having lunch, and I look up, and this kid is hanging around where the serving line starts, like he's waiting for somebody. I'm trying to stay out of sight. I'm not in uniform, which helps, but I'm on crutches, so I'm not much use."

"I'm on my way," Hood said. "Stay on the phone," he added as he turned toward the church and found his path blocked by Andrew.

"You need to do right by my boy." Andrew swayed unsteadily.

"Not now." Hood sidestepped him and ran along the street, weaving among dawdling and sauntering festival-goers. He paused at the church's side entrance, took a few deep breaths to calm his labored breathing, lifted the phone, and said, "Still with me?"

"Uh huh," Lester answered.

Hood was considering calling for backup when Lester added, "Looks like he's having second thoughts. Looks like he's getting ready to leave."

"What's he wearing?"

"Black jeans, a dark hoodie and—he's heading for the exit."

Hood reacted. To avoid any repetition of a chase or gunplay, he pushed through the side door and faced the suspect. Jet feinted right, but Hood was not fooled. He drove his shoulder into the suspect's chest and took him to the floor. In an instant, the sheriff flipped the man and pinned him beneath his bulk.

"You're under arrest."

"For what, man?"

Hood removed a handgun from a pocket of the suspect's hoodie. "You have a permit for this?" he asked.

"I know my rights, man. You can't just tackle me. You gotta have a reason."

Hood looked up and saw Lester among the onlookers who had filtered out of the cafeteria. "This the guy?" he asked his deputy, who was leaning on crutches.

"That's him."

"There's your reason," Hood told Jet. "You shot a sheriff's deputy. That's assault with a deadly weapon."

INTERLUDE:
In the Sweet By and By

Angela is determined to try again.

She turns on the phonograph and places the needle on the first song of the record, which has remained on the turntable.

Amazing grace!
How sweet the sound that saved a wretch like me!
I once was lost, but now am found
Was blind, but now I see.

Again, she sees nothing: no shapes, no colors, no images.

She plays the song to its conclusion, then lifts the needle and stares through the glass panes to the fields and hedgerows behind her house.

After what seems a long time but may only be seconds, she flips the record and replaces the phonograph needle.

In the sweet by and by
We shall meet on the beautiful shore.

Angela absorbs the hymn as she sketches the shoreline.

SENSE OF GRACE

She can almost hear her mother's voice harmonizing with the record she is playing.

She remembers her mother's voice as beautiful, then wonders if it truly was melodious or if it only seemed so to her adolescent, untrained ear.

> There's a land that is fairer than day;
> And by faith we can see it afar;
> For the Father waits over the way,
> To prepare us a dwelling-place there.

The word "father" causes her to shiver and errantly streak color where she had not intended. She cannot recall ever hearing her father sing. Or hum. Or whistle. She cannot summon a single memory of her father laughing. Or even smiling.

> To our bountiful Father above,
> We will offer our tribute of praise.
> For the glorious gift of His love,
> And the blessings that hallow our days.

Angela puts down her brush and palette. The tune is bitter. Nothing about it is sweet. She wants it to end.

She lifts the phonograph arm, removing the needle from the grooves of the record.

She looks again through the glass and stares vacantly at a fallow field. Her focus is drawn to a glint of sunlight that flashes amid the dark tangle of a distant hedgerow.

She is startled. Was the light a reflection? From what—a watch crystal, a lens, a piece of glass?

She can feel her heart beating more rapidly as she continues watching—all the time wondering if she is being watched.

CHAPTER

13

"They're ready for you," Maggie informed her boss.

"On my way," Hood said. He knew he needed to shift gears. His mind was still on Young John. He had just disconnected from the call he had made to get an update from his rookie deputy. Although Young John reported he had not yet met with a counselor, he had made an appointment for the earliest opening, which would be next week. Hood followed up with additional questions and, satisfied with the answers, offered provisional reinstatement. Young John had accepted.

Hood retrieved a file from atop his desk, left his office, and walked briskly to the interrogation room. He knocked to announce his arrival, opened the door, and experienced a *déjà vu* moment—this time with a different suspect and attorney.

Hood opened the file. "James Tyler Johnson," he read, "also known as J.T., also known as Jet." He sat and looked across the table at the young black man. "Which do you prefer, James, J.T., Jet, or something that's not listed here?"

"Jet's fine."

Hood thought the man looked younger than his age,

listed at 20. In his jail-issued coveralls—at least two sizes too large for his slender frame—he appeared boyish. His hair was short, his cheeks and chin were clean shaven, and his eyes alert.

Seated with him was long-time public defender "Only" Ray Mosley. He had acquired his nickname based on his propensity to diminish a client's culpability, as in "he's only a kid" or "he only jacked the radio; it's not like he stole the car." Only Ray appeared baffled, as if he hadn't yet figured out how to minimize shooting a deputy, and Jet's relaxed swagger struck Hood as manufactured and unconvincing.

Hood informed the two men the audio and video equipment were recording the conversation, recited the suspect's rights, and asked if they understood.

"We got it," Only Ray answered.

"Good," Hood said. He refocused on the file. "I see here an extensive history of juvenile offenses, misdemeanors and minor felonies. I also see you've served a few jail terms." He looked at Jet. "Why don't you tell me something about yourself."

"Looks like you've got all you need right there."

Hood had prepared himself to be patient. "I'm looking at a rap sheet from St. Louis. You're more than a hundred miles from home. What brings you here?"

Jet looked to his attorney, who nodded slightly, signaling it was okay to answer. Jet shrugged. "Just wanted to get out of the city."

"I get that," Hood said. "I called a captain I know there. Some people don't think big city cops and county sheriffs communicate, but we do. He connected me to a lieutenant in the gang enforcement unit."

Although Jet said nothing, he squirmed slightly in a way Hood interpreted as discomfort.

"He sent me the stuff that's listed here," Hood said, using the back of his left hand to slap the document. "He also told me you were connected with a gang called the Street Kings. Does that sound right?"

Jet looked at Only Ray. Neither replied.

"The lieutenant said your big brother had some cred with the Kings, which greased the wheels for you, but all that changed when you were involved in a drug deal that ended with no cash, no drugs, and a fellow Street King lying dead in the gutter. I can see why you wanted to get out of the city."

Although Jet retained a stoic expression, his eye movements betrayed flashes of fear.

Hood stared at Jet. When the young man met his gaze, Hood asked, "Do the Kings know you're here in Huhman County?"

"Just what are you implying?" Only Ray asked.

Hood shrugged, purposely. "I'm not implying anything. I'm just making an observation. Jet's got a bit of a record, but he's mostly managed to stay out of big trouble. Not anymore. He shot a sheriff's deputy. He's got gang trouble, and he's got law enforcement trouble. If I was between that rock and that hard place, I'd be looking to make the best deal I could."

* * * * *

Hood put his hands in his pockets to wipe the sweat from his palms.

He had anticipated he would feel anxious, but not to this degree. He considered it ironic that a simple conversation or meeting could create greater unease than facing an armed felon.

He looked again at his clock—8:56 a.m.—and wondered if Angela would arrive on time. He had made a morning appointment to minimize his expected discomfort, but the strategy failed; his anxiety began the night before and created a patchwork of sleep disruptions.

The ringing of his desk phone startled him. "Angela Grace is here," Maggie informed him.

"I'll come out," he said.

He arose from his desk and opened the window blinds. He attempted to check his teeth—again, he had inspected himself in the men's room mirror only minutes ago—but the window glass offered no reflection, only a view of autumn leaves falling intermittently on the courthouse lawn. He scolded himself for his juvenile behavior but straightened his uniform before leaving his office to greet her.

A flexible, white plastic mask outlined the contours of Angela's face, concealing the features below her steel-blue eyes. Hood recalled the magazine photos and wondered if she chose the more secure accessory for public venues. Her daffodil yellow hair fell along the shoulders and back of a nut-brown sweater she wore with fitted blue jeans and brown suede walking shoes. Prince stood beside her.

The sheriff and Angela exchanged greetings and, with her permission, Hood knelt and petted Prince.

"May we talk, in private?" Angela asked.

"Of course." Hood arose. "Follow me."

Angela sat in one of the visitor chairs, and Hood opted to do the same, a gesture designed to make their visit seem more casual and less official. Prince sat on the floor between them.

"Thank you for seeing me," Angela said. "I know you're busy, so I'll get right to the point. I think someone may be watching me. It happened twice yesterday, during the day and again after dark."

Hood nodded.

"In the afternoon, I was painting in my studio—the room at the back of the house that captures all the natural light—and I saw a glint, like a reflection from something. It came from a hedgerow bordering a field behind my house."

"A hunter, a hiker, some kids?" Hood surmised.

"That's what I thought, too," she said. "So Prince and I walked back there and found nothing." Angela paused. "I figured it was like you said, maybe somebody wandering around back there, but I looked out the window again in the evening, before dark—I couldn't help myself—and I swear I saw a movement coming from the same place. That's when I called and made the appointment. I thought I should report it."

"I'm glad you did, but you didn't have to come here. I would have come to you."

"I feel like some kid imagining a monster in the closet. But

I saw what I saw, and—I know this is not, like, hard evidence—
but I just have this creepy feeling that I'm being watched."

"Do you have any idea who it could be?"

"Not really."

"Do you think it could be your father?"

"It crossed my mind. After all, I'm the prime suspect in
the assaults. You think so. Maybe he does, too. Maybe he's
keeping an eye on me."

Hood pondered her words. A part of him wanted to
assure her she was not the prime suspect, but he knew that
wasn't true. If anything, he was uncertain. "I have another
thought," he said.

"I'm listening."

"I'm not sure how to broach this exactly."

"I swear, sometimes you treat me like I'm so fragile, so
breakable. I assure you, Sheriff, after what I've been through,
I won't shatter into a million pieces."

"Do you wear a mask or a veil all the time?"

"Except when I sleep."

"When you paint?"

"Yes. Typically, the veil. Ah," she said, suddenly grasping
his suspicions. "You think somebody might be trying to see my
face."

"Or photograph you without the mask. Are there any
pictures of you since the—" he began, his question interrupted
by the ring of his desk phone. The light indicated the caller
was Maggie. Hood knew she would interrupt only if she
considered it necessary.

SENSE OF GRACE

"I'd better get this," he said then lifted the receiver.

"Sorry to bother you, but your wife is here," Maggie said. "Apparently, your daughter's been in some trouble at school."

"I'll be right out." He replaced the receiver, and said to Angela, "Sorry, I've got to go. Family matter."

"I understand."

Hood followed Angela and Prince out of his office and saw his wife standing near the dispatch station. Hood noticed his wife's quizzical expression. He overtook Angela, placed himself between the two women, and introduced them to each other.

"A pleasure to meet you," Angela said. Her tone was gracious, but she did not extend her hand. "Your husband has been very helpful during this—" She shrugged. "I'm not even sure what to call it."

"Case," Hood interjected.

"Nice to meet you, too," Linda said to Angela. She turned to her husband. "I need to talk to you."

"I was just leaving," Angela said.

"I'll call you," Hood said to Angela as she and Prince turned to leave, "to arrange a time when I can come out and take a look." As they walked away, he looked at his wife. "What's up?"

"The school called. Elizabeth got in a fight with another girl. I—"

"Is she okay?"

"She's fine. I called your cell, but got your voice mail. I just stopped by to see if you wanted to come—"

"Of course I do." Hood removed his phone and switched it to ring. "I just turned the cell off—"

"You don't need to explain."

Hood sensed the tension in her tone. "I'd better take the cruiser in case—"

"Can we just go?"

"Sure."

Hood followed his wife to the school and caught up with her in the parking lot. "When did this happen? Did the school say what the fight was about?"

"That's what we're here to find out."

They walked together to the school's administrative offices, where they waited briefly before being met by the principal, who greeted Linda warmly, then introduced herself to Hood as Mrs. Jeffries. The obvious parent-educator bond between the two women reminded him of his comparative lack of involvement in Elizabeth's school activities.

Mrs. Jeffries, who didn't witness the incident, outlined what she had learned from second-hand reports, which Hood immediately downplayed as hearsay. Elizabeth and a classmate argued—neither would disclose the subject—in a school corridor and were observed trading slap punches and wrestling each other to the floor. Neither was injured. Hood wondered if—in this age of hypersensitivity to confrontation and bullying—the educators overreacted to a garden-variety, schoolyard spat.

"Have either of you," Mrs. Jeffries asked, "noticed a change in Elizabeth's behavior, or are you aware of any circumstances that may be affecting her mood or attitude?"

Hood was about to say "no" when Linda answered. "We've been dealing with some family issues lately. That may be part of it. I don't know. I'll talk to her."

Hood was both dismayed by what his wife had shared and relieved by her lack of specifics. When Mrs. Jeffries focused on him, he nodded agreement. At that moment, he felt out of touch with his family and powerless to do anything about it. He simply wanted the meeting to end.

As if on cue, his cell phone rang. He removed it and glanced at the display, indicating the call was from the prosecutor's office.

"Do you need to—?" Mrs. Jeffries began.

"I can call back," Hood said.

"Well," Mrs. Jeffries said. "I think we're done here. I'm going to issue Elizabeth a warning, but no punishment. This was her first disciplinary issue, but I can't be so lenient if it continues. I hope you'll help prevent any recurrence."

"Absolutely," Linda agreed.

"Of course," Hood added.

Hood and Linda left the school and walked together across the parking lot.

"This isn't like Elizabeth," Hood said. "To get into trouble, I mean."

Linda didn't reply.

When they reached her car, he opened the door for her. "Think she's acting out because of us—the separation, I mean?" he asked.

"Now's not the time," Linda said. She got into the driver's seat, started the car, and drove away.

"Hi, I'm Chris and I'm an alcoholic."

Hood joined the "Hi Chris" chorus. He was among about a dozen people gathered around the tables in the church basement for Matthew's meeting. Hood hadn't missed a weekly meeting since he began attending more than two months ago. He hadn't seen Chris before—the young man's short hair, wire-rimmed glasses, and long beard were distinctive—but Hood had learned not to equate sporadic attendance with time in recovery.

"I'm confused," Chris continued. "Is my higher power some external, omnipotent entity or something inside me? I hear people in recovery say: 'There is a God and it isn't you' or 'let go and let God.' Then somebody else seems to contradict that by saying: 'This is a spiritual program of action.'

"So do I let go or take action? The other day I was reading this meditation by a Christian theologian, and he suggested God is within every human being. He went so far as to say we're not human beings seeking spirituality; we're spiritual beings having a human experience.

"If I'm supposed to improve my relationship with God, where do I look—out there somewhere or inside myself?" He paused. "Pass."

"Jenny," Matthew prompted.

"Jenny, alcoholic." When the group's greeting subsided,

she said, "You come up with the weirdest shit, Chris. All I know is I'm not God, I'm not even sure I'm a believer. But today I'm sober and that's somethin' for me to hold on to. I pass to Mac."

"Hi, I'm Mac. I'm an alcoholic."

Hood had become acclimated to the group greeting for each speaker, which initially had seemed strange and ritualistic.

"For me, it's both," Mac said. "You know, I didn't come here to find salvation: I came here to get sober. But the more time I spent around spiritual people talking about what spirituality means, the more my life changed. As an alcoholic, I was lonely and miserable. Today, I appreciate and enjoy life.

"For me, what Chris is talking about isn't a weird concept at all. The foundation of some major religions is an all-knowing, all-seeing, external deity. And in Christianity, for example, as I understand it—there's the idea of Christ being in me and me in Christ."

Mac paused briefly. "I may never understand what my higher power has in store for me in the afterlife," he added. "But I've experienced a miraculous transformation in finding a faith that works in daily living. I'll pass to Francis."

Hood looked at people focused on him. "Hi, my name's Francis, and I'm an alcoholic. I think I'm just going to listen and learn tonight."

After the meeting ended and the attendees dispersed, Hood lingered in the basement. He helped Matthew dump coffee grounds, rinse coffee pots, and stack folding chairs.

As they finished the chores, Matthew asked, "What's on your mind, Francis?"

"Is it that obvious?"

"You seem preoccupied. Want to talk about it?"

"People in the program are always saying, 'Do the next right thing,' but I've got this situation where I'm not sure what that is."

Matthew unfolded two chairs, sat, and gestured for Hood to join him.

"Well," Hood continued, moving his chair to face Matthew directly, "I've got this deputy who I think may have a drinking problem and I'm not sure whether to tell him I do too."

"That's a tough one," Matthew said. "What's your gut tell you?"

"That's the problem. I like this kid, and part of me wants to let him know he's not alone. But professionally, I'm his boss, and I've got to look out for what's best for the department. I've already put him on leave. But if it turns out he does have a problem and doesn't get help, I may have to discipline him further. Maybe even fire him."

"Has he reached out to you for help?"

"Not really. I've asked him to see a counselor through our Employee Assistance Program, and he's set up an appointment."

"Did he seem reluctant or eager about the opportunity?"

Hood considered before answering. "Mostly reluctant. I'm not sure he thinks he has a problem."

"Well," Matthew said, "Our program asks us to be available when people recognize they have a problem and ask for help. Sadly, a lot of people either don't recognize it or don't want to recognize it. You've probably heard the slogan that recovery is for people who want it, not people who need it."

"So," Hood said, "you're telling me to say nothing—at least not yet."

"That has to be your decision." Matthew said. "You have a much better understanding of the situation, the deputy,— and yourself."

"I keep going back and forth," Hood said. "But I've still got these reservations about telling him I'm an alcoholic. I'm not sure why, but I'm pretty sure there's a reason." They sat silently for a time before Hood added, "I guess I just answered my own question."

CHAPTER

14

Hood bent toward the ground and swept the toe of his boot through the tall, wispy weeds, seeking evidence.

He had found nothing to suggest someone had been watching Angela from the hedgerow. Although his expectations ebbed, his inspection remained deliberate.

"You think this is the spot?" he asked, seeking confirmation from Angela, who stood, with Prince beside her, on a nearby rutted road separating the overgrowth from a fallow field.

"Yes. I used that red bush to identify the area where I saw the reflection." She pointed to a crimson shrub near Hood's feet.

He resumed his search.

"Everything work out yesterday?" Angela asked.

Hood looked at her. "How do you mean?"

"Your wife seemed—what's the word?—distracted."

Hood was surprised. He hadn't expected Angela to pick up on—or give any thought to—Linda's mood. Hood knew his wife was unnerved about the fight involving their daughter, but some contributing factor had amplified her annoyance. "Elizabeth got in some trouble at school," he said. "It all worked out."

"Elizabeth is your daughter?"

Hood nodded.

"How old is she?"

"Fourteen. She's a freshman."

"How many children do you have?"

"Just the one." Hood stooped over and poked his index finger among dried leaves, twigs, and acorns.

"How long have you and Linda been married?"

"We celebrated our—wait, what's this?"

"What?"

"Looks like a toothpick." Hood took tweezers and a small, clear plastic bag from a pocket, carefully grasped the wooden object between the pincers, and examined it. His brain automatically conjured an image of Randy Knaebel with a wooden toothpick in his mouth in the same moment Angela said, "Randy was chewing a toothpick the other day."

"Let's not get ahead of ourselves," Hood dropped the toothpick into the bag and sealed it. Although he was encouraged to find a potential clue, he also knew the folly of rash conclusions. "I'll have the lab test it, and we'll go from there." He continued his search, gradually widening the circle from where he made the find.

After a lengthy silence, Angela asked, "What are you thinking right now?"

"What makes you think I'm thinking anything?"

"Something's on your mind," she persisted. "I can tell."

"Okay," Hood said. "What's on my mind is your uncanny

ability to sense when people have something on their mind." He paused. "Does that come with the—what is it—synesthesion thing?"

"Synesthesia," she corrected. "And, no, so far as I know, it doesn't. I just know when people aren't telling me what they're thinking." She looked away across the field, then refocused on Hood. "For example, I know when people look at me and wonder what's under the veil. I know that's my fault; I hide myself. I also know for some people it's just morbid curiosity, but that's not true of everybody. Every once in a while, I meet someone who seems interested in who I really am." She stopped abruptly. "But I'm talking too much."

Hood looked at her. He was unsure what to say. They faced each other in silence amid the sounds of squirrels scurrying from tree to tree, rattling withering leaves, while a blue jay scolded from a branch overhead.

"We're losing the light," Hood said. "May as well head back."

They walked together along the rutted road, facing a sunset reminiscent of images people capture on cell phones and post on social media, often with an inspirational quotation or verse from scripture.

"Ever paint anything like that?" Hood asked, as he studied nature's feathery strokes of violet, yellow, and orange above the darkening horizon.

"Not my style," Angela answered, dismissively.

"Too . . . ?" He drew out the word, hoping she would fill in the blank.

"Too what? Too mainstream, too pedestrian? What do you want me to say?"

Hood shrugged. "Some people would say it's heavenly."

"That's fine if you believe in heaven."

"But you don't?"

"Do you?"

"I believe in something, but not the standard images of God with a white beard, Christ on the cross, or heaven as a white, sunlit city."

"So artists are just liars?" she asked, with no hint of being offended.

"They're interpreting what they can't see. Or know. Now, with a sunset, it's right there. It's beautiful."

"Beauty lost its allure for me a long time ago."

Hood stopped walking.

She did, too. "What?"

He considered saying something complimentary about her resilience, her fortitude, her ability to adapt. "Never mind." He resumed walking.

When they reached the back of her house, a battered Olds Cutlass was parked in the driveway. Behind the wheel was Randy Knaebel.

"Speak of the devil," Hood said. He noticed a trace of surprise in Angela's widened eyes.

"I'd better see what he wants," she said as Randy got out of his car. A wooden toothpick protruded from his lips.

As Randy approached, Angela said, "I wasn't expecting you," then added, "the sheriff and I were just following up on something."

"Looking for evidence," Hood said.

"Evidence?" Randy asked.

"Angela has reason to believe someone may be watching her," Hood responded, preempting any comment from her. Hood adopted a conversational tone to mask his intent—to see if Randy would react. He detected nothing but mild surprise. "Say, can I have one of those toothpicks?"

"Sure," Randy said. He took a small box from his pocket, removed a toothpick and handed it to the sheriff.

"Thanks." Hood turned his attention to Angela. "Well, I'd better get going. There's work to be done. I'll be in touch."

"Thanks again, Sheriff," Angela said, as he walked to his cruiser.

"So," Angela said to Randy as the sheriff drove away, "what brings you here?"

"Just came to visit." He shrugged awkwardly. "I enjoyed catching up the other day."

"Me, too. Want something to drink?"

"Sure."

Randy followed Angela inside and into the kitchen, where Odessa was dipping a silver tea ball into a steaming pot. "Just made some chamomile," Odessa said. She looked up and saw Randy. "Where's the sheriff?"

"He had to leave," Angela replied.

"Well, there's tea," Odessa said. She poured some for herself and left the kitchen.

Angela walked to the counter. "I can make some fresh coffee."

162

"Tea's fine."

When they were settled across from each other at the table, each with a cup of tea, Randy said, "So, I was just wondering—after we spoke, I mean—you must be pretty busy with your art and your students, and the fundraising, and all."

"I stay pretty busy, especially when I have a show coming up. But Odessa's a big help, and Ethan, so it's manageable unless I hear something that inspires me. Then I can get pretty manic for a while."

"Hear something?" Randy asked, obviously puzzled.

"Sorry, I just assumed you knew. I have a neurological condition called synesthesia. My brain translates certain sounds into images and colors for me and, sometimes, I get into this obsessive-compulsive painting mode. I've been known to go without food, sleep, whatever, until I'm satisfied I've captured the sensation in a finished artwork." She sipped tea through a straw.

"Wow. Are you musical? Do you play an instrument?"

"No."

"Me neither." He grinned as he held up his mittened hand.

"I've always liked that about you. You always seemed okay with who you are."

Randy shrugged and repositioned the toothpick. "Just had to find a way to deal with it. I had some surgeries when I was a kid, my dad being who he is and all, but things just didn't . . . " He left the sentence incomplete.

"Me, too—surgeries, I mean—when I was younger," Angela said. "But my face didn't look real to me. My guardians were willing to do anything to continue, but I didn't want to. I begged them to stop."

"I wonder sometimes if it's easier for me. Being born with it, I mean."

"I don't know. It's like you said: we learn to deal with it, to adapt. At least people don't call us freaks anymore, like when we were kids."

"Not to our faces, at least."

Silence ensued. Angela sipped more tea, noting Randy's cup remained untouched.

"So," Randy said, "I was wondering: do you go out much?"

"Depends."

"On?"

"Well, if I'm opening an exhibit, it's expected. Therefore, I do it, but I don't like it much. I don't like being the center of attention. I mean, I know I'm there so people can talk to me, interact with me, but I still feel self-conscious. It's weird. It's like I wear a mask so that people won't look at me, but that's why they look at me."

"Same with my mitten," Randy said. "Do you ever go out, like, to a movie or something?"

Angela laughed briefly. "I can't even remember the last time I did that."

"Would you like to? Go to a movie, I mean, with me?"

Angela sipped tea. "Thanks, but I don't think so."

"It doesn't have to be a movie. We could just go, I don't know . . . "

"Don't misunderstand," Angela said. "I'm glad we

reconnected. And if you want to get together once in a while to chat—as friends, like we're doing now—that's fine. But you probably should call first, make sure I'm here, rather than just stopping by."

As the two deputies climbed out of the cruiser, they heard shouting coming from inside the house.

"I know these folks," Wally said to Young John, who was serving his first shift since being reinstated by the sheriff. "They scream like banshees, but they're pretty harmless."

Young John nodded as they approached the house, a well-maintained Dutch Colonial in a middle-class subdivision.

Wally knocked on the front door. The clamor inside continued.

Wally knocked again, more forcefully.

The caterwauling stopped. "Who is it?" a voice called.

Wally recognized Glenn Neuner's voice. "Sheriff"'s department," Wally announced. "Glenn, it's me. Wally."

Glenn opened the door and stepped outside. "Is there a problem?" he asked, confrontation still evident in his tone.

Glenn's wife, Teresa, appeared in the open doorway. "He's the problem," she snarled, pointing to her husband. "Go 'head and take him away, Wally, 'cause he ain't doin' me no good."

Glenn turned and faced her. "You're the goddamn problem. I don't know why I—"

"Enough," Wally ordered. "We received a report of a

domestic disturbance and you—"

"Goddamn neighbors," Glenn snapped.

"Ought to mind their own goddamn business," Teresa added.

"You two need to cool down," Wally said. He glanced at Young John, who smirked at the couple's obvious intoxication.

"Tell him to cool down," Teresa said, pointing at her husband. "He's the one's been doin' all the shoutin'."

"I'm shouting so you can hear me over your goddamn shouting."

Wally held up his hand in a halting gesture. "Okay, stop. Both of you." He paused to be certain he had their attention. "You know the rules. If you don't cool off and we have to come back a second time, somebody's going to jail. That's the law."

"She's the one who ought to be going to jail," Glenn said. "She's the one doing the goddamn shouting."

"I'm not shoutin' and I'm not goin' to jail," Teresa retorted. "Just haul this old fart's ass to jail right now and save yourself a trip."

"Wally ain't hauling my ass to jail because he knows you're the one—"

"Enough!" Young John shouted. His abrupt entry into the confrontation silenced everyone. "Not another word from either of you or we'll haul both your asses to jail."

"You can't talk to my wife like that," Glenn said.

Young John stepped forward, spun Glenn around where he stood, and reached for his handcuffs.

"Let go of my husband," Teresa hollered. She stepped

outside, pushed Young John, and kicked at his shins.

Chaos ensued as Teresa jumped on the rookie deputy's back and began pummeling him as he tried to cuff her husband, while Wally pulled at the combatants in a vain attempt to separate them and restore order.

CHAPTER

15

"Got a minute?" Hood asked his chief deputy, who was refilling his coffee cup.

Wally knew from experience the question was a summons. "Sure," he said. "Your office?"

"Please."

When they were seated and the door was closed, Hood said, "Want to tell me why the county is paying room and board for Glenn and Teresa Neuner?"

"It's, um, as I put in my report, we were—"

"I read the report." Hood lifted it from the center of his desk and held it momentarily before letting it drop. "They're in their seventies, and they drink too much, and they shout at each other too loud and too often but, to my knowledge, they've never laid a hand on one another."

Wally looked down at his shoes. "I guess things kinda got out of control."

"How exactly did they get out of control?"

Wally hesitated for a long moment. He wasn't surprised by his boss's reaction. He had replayed the scenario several times and accepted responsibility. He was, after all, the veteran partner on the scene, and he had no intention of shifting blame to Young John. "I don't know," he answered. "They just did."

"How many times have you responded to a disturbance at their house?"

"I don't know—four or five."

"And it's always the same thing, right? The same neighbor makes the same complaint. We respond, warn them we have to arrest one of them if we have to come back, and they calm down. How was this time any different?"

Wally shrugged.

"Your report said they were arrested for failure to obey a reasonable order and for resisting arrest."

Wally nodded.

"Who tried to arrest them, you or Young John?"

"The bottom line is I—"

"You don't have to answer. I already know. I knew when I read your report you were covering for Young John. What kind of shape was he in?"

"I'm not sure I know what you mean."

"Was he acting normal? Was he moody, combative?"

"I don't know. He seemed okay to me. A little preoccupied, maybe."

"Preoccupied?"

"A little. Like there were other things on his mind."

"Could you tell if he'd been drinking?"

"Drinking?" Wally repeated, surprised by the question.

"Yes. Did he seem impaired? Did you smell alcohol on

his breath?"

"No," Wally said. He paused momentarily, then added, "You think Young John's been drinking on the job?"

"Just covering all the bases."

"I don't think so," Wally said. "It was just, you know, one thing led to another, and then all hell broke loose."

Randy rapped on the rear door of the abandoned service station. No one answered. He looked around the property. No activity.

He was familiar with the premises. As a child, he would tell his mom he was going to a friend's house, then sneak through several neighborhood back yards to Eddie's Texaco. At age seven, he was obsessed with earth-moving equipment and trucks, and Eddie, the station owner, also operated a towing service. Randy and Eddie became friends and, during idle times at the station, Eddie would buy the boy a bottle of Coke and let him drink it while he sat behind the wheel of the tow truck.

Those times at the station were among Randy's fondest childhood memories, so he was saddened—after his return to Huhman County as an adult—to find Eddie's Texaco closed. When he considered a place to hide Jet, however, the shuttered station immediately came to mind. On the initial visit, he and Jet had to break in the back door. This time, Randy twisted the doorknob and found it unlocked.

He entered and, in the dim light afforded by the windows,

watched a critter—a rat, perhaps?—scurry from the office to a garage bay. Randy unshouldered a rucksack of supplies—including canned meat, wine, toilet paper, some pot—and set it on a counter. He gnawed his trademark toothpick while he made a mental note to bring some rat traps and, maybe, some insect spray. Who knows, he wondered, what creatures had moved in since the building was vacated, likely some years ago?

Randy sensed the interior was more than quiet; it was vacant. He remained still, listening for the slightest sound. "Jet?" he called.

No response.

"Son of a bitch," he whispered aloud, aggravated that Jet had not followed his instructions to stay put.

Then another thought rushed into his brain: what if the Street Kings had found him?

It was unlikely, but again he tuned his senses to any activity. After a time, he searched the interior of the station.

No one else was within, and no note explained where Jet had gone.

Hood looked alternately at the two red and white plastic bobbers sitting motionless on the tranquil surface of the farm pond. On the far shore, a gaggle of geese waddled and quarreled, while his daughter, who sat beside him, tapped a text message on her cell phone.

Hood, who had become more sensitive to sounds since

meeting Angela, found the clashing noises discordant and irksome. "You're not watching your bobber," Hood said.

"I just need to send this to Claire," Elizabeth replied, without looking away from the screen.

Hood said nothing. He reminded himself not to adopt his daughter's sullen mood. And he tried not to appear impatient as he waited until she put away her phone. "What are you thinking?" Hood asked.

"I'm just waiting for the lecture. Can we just get it over with?"

"What makes you think I'm going to lecture you?"

"Because of what happened at school. Isn't that why we're here?"

"No," Hood said. "Your mom told me you had a day off because of some teacher training, so I asked you if you wanted to go fishing with me. I thought it would be fun. Remember how you used to enjoy it?"

"I was, like, eleven."

Three years, Hood thought, might not be a long time for adults, but must seem a millennium for adolescents. "I just wanted us to spend some time together."

"So you're not going to scold me, tell me I'm screwing up my life?"

The question put Hood on a high wire, balancing his responsibilities as a parent and his awareness of his shortcomings as an alcoholic. "Elizabeth, I'm sorry your mom and I are separated right now. That's on me. It's not her fault and it's certainly not yours."

She focused on the bobber and said nothing.

"My drinking got out of control," he continued. "I didn't mean for it to happen, but it did. And it got to the point where if I wasn't drinking, I was thinking about it. It was in my head all the time, and the only way to stop thinking about it was to do it."

Elizabeth faced him and he saw in her expression that she was puzzled, confused.

"It's difficult for people who don't have an addiction to understand what it's like. That's why I've been going to meetings—to talk to other alcoholics because they understand what it's like."

"So, are you okay now?"

"As long as I don't drink." He paused. "But I'm an alcoholic. If I take a drink it all starts up again, and I'll be back where I was. I tried to deny that for a long time; I tried to convince myself my drinking didn't hurt anyone else. But now I know it did. That's the truth—a sad and painful truth. I can't lie to you, to your mom, or to myself anymore."

"Are you and Mom getting back together?"

"I hope so. It may take some time. I realize that I damaged my relationship with your mom and with you. I want to do what I can to repair the damage and rebuild trust. I know I need to change."

"Change how?"

"I'm not sure I know the answer right now," he said. "That's what I'm finding out. I'm trying to figure out how to deal with life—with people, with situations, with everything—

without turning to alcohol. People in the program call it dealing with life on life's terms."

"Damn," Elizabeth shouted as she leaned back and yanked on the fishing rod.

Hood thought she was reacting to his words until he saw the tip of her rod bending and twitching. "Looks like a good-sized fish," he said.

Elizabeth stood. She surprised herself by remembering how to adjust the drag on the reel so the fish wouldn't break the line.

Hood was impressed. He guessed by the action of the rod tip that the fish was a bass, probably a largemouth. "Keep the line taut. Wear him out."

She followed instructions. When the action slowed, she began to reel in line while Hood readied the landing net.

In an instant, it was over. The line went slack, the fish was gone, and Hood and his daughter stared at the pond surface in disbelief.

"I don't know what happened," Elizabeth said as she reeled in the line. "I thought I had it hooked pretty good."

Hood shrugged. Life on life's terms, he thought.

"Got a minute?" Maggie asked her boss, as she stood in the door frame of his office.

Hood looked up and smiled. He wondered if she knew she had borrowed his line for summoning people. "Sure," he said. "I've got an appointment with the prosecutor, but that's later today."

Maggie closed the door, sat on the edge of a visitor's chair, and leaned forward but said nothing.

Hood focused on her, listening but not prompting.

"Francis, I've been around awhile, and the one thing I've noticed is sometimes men don't know much about women."

Hood narrowed his eyes, pursed his lips. Among all the potential topics he suspected might be on Maggie's mind, he was surprised.

"I, uh," Maggie continued, "was at my station the other day when you introduced Angela to Linda and I couldn't help . . . I sensed some friction. I just want you to be careful—"

"Angela is just a part of this case I'm working on," he interrupted. "In fact, she's a suspect, although she also may be a stalking victim. I'm just trying—" This time he stopped himself. He saw, in Maggie's expression, that he sounded defensive. Was he trying, he wondered, to convince her or himself? He knew he had been trying to sort out his complicated connection to Angela Grace, just as he was attempting to assess the damage done to his relationship with Linda. He had always thought of Linda not only as his wife, but as his world. Was that world coming to an end? Was he grasping, in some convoluted way, to form a new attachment?

"I know you don't mean to hurt anyone," Maggie said, softly. "But you're going through a tough time right now, in more ways than one."

Hood nodded agreement.

"Please be careful," Maggie added. "You know what's in

your heart, but that's not always apparent to the people around you."

Hood was quiet, contemplative.

"That's all," Maggie said, almost a whisper.

She arose and was nearly out the door when Hood said, "Thanks."

Hood sat in a visitor's chair facing the impeccably dressed and well-groomed county prosecutor, Leonardo "Leo" Pancrazio.

Leo was not a native of Huhman County. He was one of three sons of a patriarch who had built a successful family-owned business distributing spirits—liquor, wine, and beer—in Kansas City and its environs. Although his place in the company was assured, he opted instead to pursue a career in criminal justice—much to the dismay of his father and brothers.

After law school he was recruited to join the prosecutor's staff, and when his boss decided to retire to a more lucrative private practice, Leo was encouraged to seek election to the office. Relying on his oratory skills, polished presence, and superb courtroom record, he won handily.

"Got a call from Only Ray Mosley at the public defender's office," Leo began. "He said he was there when you interviewed one of his clients"—he glanced at a document on his desk—"this J.T. Johnson fellow."

Hood nodded.

"I don't know what you said, but you got their attention."

"His client—he goes by Jet—got sideways with a St. Louis gang called the Street Kings. If they find him, it'll be worse than anything we throw at him."

Leo nodded. "Only Ray wants to know if we're willing to negotiate."

Hood appreciated Leo's use of the "we" pronoun. Hood knew prosecutors exercise enormous discretion concerning what criminal charges, if any, are filed. Although they are not obligated to confer with other law enforcement officials, Leo routinely consulted the arresting officers before moving forward. He also consulted them before hammering out plea bargains or recommending punishments. But, ultimately, Leo made his own decisions, not to placate law enforcement or to pad his win-loss record, but to pursue justice.

"What're they offering?" Hood asked.

"Only Ray said his client can help clear some other crimes."

"What crimes?"

"He's not showing any cards yet. And I have no idea what he wants, although from what you said, I'm guessing the safety of his client is on the list. What Only Ray wants to know first is whether we're willing to come to the table."

"That kid shot my deputy."

"That's why he's not showing any cards. He wants to see if we're flexible. Look, Francis, if you want to take a hard line on this, I'm in. I'll argue attempted murder of a law enforcement officer during the commission of a felony drug transaction, but . . . " Leo leaned back, "Only Ray has been at this a long time. He knows that'll be a tough sell. I read Lester's report. He said the kid hardly looked back, he just fired. That leaves assault with a deadly weapon, maybe armed criminal action. Those are still serious charges, but what I'm saying is we've got some negotiating room if you want me to explore that."

Hood sat silently for a moment. "I need to talk to Lester first."

Leo shrugged. "Fine, but we both know what Lester will say. He'll say, 'What's done is done. Why not get something worthwhile out of it?'"

"I know," Hood said, "but I still need to talk to him."

"I understand," Leo said. "The sooner, the better."

Hood checked in at Missouri Highway Patrol headquarters, clipped the visitor's badge to his uniform, and walked briskly to the crime lab.

When he entered, Sandra was tapping a keyboard and intensely watching a computer monitor. She arose from her chair and greeted him. He had called ahead, and she was expecting him. He had worked with her on a number of cases and asked for her whenever he needed assistance.

Sandra was without artifice, personally and professionally. She used minimal makeup and gathered her long, tawny hair into a simple ponytail, but the impression she created was simultaneously natural and breathtaking. She even wore her shapeless, white lab coat in a manner that conveyed poise and elegance. But what Hood found most captivating was the scientific rigor she applied to every aspect of her life—a quality that earned her the crude nickname "No Bullshit" Sandra.

Hood reached into his shirt pocket and retrieved the plastic bag containing the toothpick. Sandra took the bag and visually examined the toothpick. "New or used?"

"That's what I'm here to find out."

"Can you give me some context?"

"Found it behind the house of a suspect who thinks she's being watched. Could belong to someone else involved in the case."

"Are you wanting a DNA test?"

Hood nodded.

Sandra frowned. "You know I'll need a written request from you and authorization from my boss before I can do that."

"Bureaucracy," Hood muttered. "I thought maybe you could cut through some red tape."

"Would if I could, but it's expensive, and we're backed up," she said. "I'll try to move you up in the order if I can, but first let me see if it's been used."

"Okay," Hood removed a second toothpick from a pants pocket. "This one should be unused. I'd also like to know if both are from the same manufacturer."

"Simple enough." She took the item, bagged it, and marked the bag. "Anything else?"

"No."

Sandra returned to her computer station and resumed

typing commands. Hood lingered expectantly. After a few moments, she looked up. "I can't do it right now, Francis. Bureaucracy sets my priorities. I'll call you tomorrow, no later." Hood smiled. He left.

"I made a mistake," Hood said.

"What do you mean?" Young John asked.

"I'm putting you back on suspension. I shouldn't have reinstated you so soon."

"Look, if this is about what happened with that drunken couple the other night—"

"I have no confidence in your judgment right now," Hood said. "I shouldn't have—"

"They were out of line. They were loud, obnoxious, they wouldn't listen to what Wally was telling—"

"It's not about that," Hood said. "It's my fault. I brought you back too soon, and now it's my responsibility to fix it."

Young John knew the decision was irrevocable. "Suspended for how long?"

"At least until you've seen a counselor. I need to regain some assurance—"

"What am I gonna tell my father?"

"I don't know that you have to tell him anything."

"He'll know," Young John whispered.

Hood was puzzled; he would have thought his deputy would be more worried about his wife's reaction. He wondered about the bizarre bond between father and son, and about

180

Andrew Bunch's chronic discontent. And he couldn't help but wonder if Andrew—the older brother of Ruth Grace, Angela's mother—was somehow involved in the attacks on Jacob.

"Lester," Hood said, "got a question for you."

"Shoot."

Hood smiled at the irony of his remark. "I hate to make you get up, but we probably should do this in private."

"Sure." Lester stood, positioned his crutches and hobbled to Hood's office.

When they were settled, Hood said, "I met with Leo, who had a visit from Only Ray, who's representing the kid who shot you. Only Ray says this Jet kid's got information on other crimes and is willing to make a deal."

"Great," Lester said, without hesitation.

Hood was not surprised. "I have no idea what the kid knows or what kind of deal we're talking about."

"I trust you and Leo."

"I told Leo I needed to talk to you first," Hood said, feeling a need to explain further. "I mean, I don't like making deals with people who shoot cops."

"You know, I really can't say he shot *at* me. He didn't even aim. I was chasing him and caught a ricochet."

"Okay. I'll tell Leo to pursue a deal."

Lester nodded. "Anything else, boss?"

"No."

As Lester returned to his desk, Hood thought about his recovery program's insistence on letting go of resentments. Lester wasn't in the program but seemed incapable of harboring ill will. Hood wondered if, with practice, he could enjoy similar peace of mind.

Bunch Farm and Home had operated in Huhman County for generations. Hood knew little about its origins but was aware of the town gossip suggesting its long run might be nearing an end.

The profit margin had dwindled over the years, attributed partially to the transition from family to corporate farm operations and partially to Andrew's generally surly attitude. In addition, Andrew's only son had veered from the legacy to law enforcement.

Feed and fencing, tools and farm toys, coveralls and durable clothing were the store's stock and trade, and the first thing Hood noticed when he entered were displays to promote seasonal sales. With hunting season approaching, insulated outerwear, including coats in safety orange and camouflage, hung on racks near checkout counters. Stock-tank warmers were stacked on a rectangular table, and a glass case displayed an array of knives, lock-back and fixed blade with serrations and gut hooks.

"May I help you?" a cashier asked, her tone courteous.

"I'm your sheriff, Francis Hood. Is Andrew Bunch available?"

"I think so." She picked up a phone.

Hood waited, revisiting his disappointment when he learned from Sandra that both toothpicks were unused. He wondered whether the object had been dropped carelessly by Randy Knaebel or someone else had placed it there to implicate Randy.

The cashier conversed briefly on the phone, hung up, and directed the sheriff to a hallway that led to restrooms, an employee break room, and, at the end, an office where Andrew stood.

"What brings you out here?" Andrew asked.

"Got a question or two," Hood glanced into the break room. "Any coffee in there?"

"Yeah." Andrew filled two disposable cups with coffee, then led Hood to his cluttered office and sat behind a metal desk. Hood sat in a visitor's chair with a torn cushion and sipped coffee, which was more flavorful than he anticipated.

"If you're expecting an apology, I'm—"

Hood held up a hand in a halting gesture. "I'm here about Jacob Grace. You know he's out of prison, right?"

"Fuck, yeah," Andrew said. "I got a victim-impact form from Corrections before they turned him loose. They said I could come to a hearing and speak, you know, 'cause I'm Ruthie's brother. So I went. And I told them that son-of-bitch ought never be set free, not after what he did to Ruthie and those kids. Course, they didn't listen."

"Did you know Jacob's been assaulted twice since he got out?"

"Heard he got his ear cut off."

Hood nodded. "He was assaulted again; someone cut off the tip of his nose."

"Should've just put the bastard out of his misery."

"That's why I'm here. I know there's no love lost—"

"You gotta be fuckin' kiddin' me, Francis," Andrew said. "How long we known each other?"

"Since we were kids."

"And you know I'm a straight shooter. I tell it like it is, and I'll tell you to your face, but I don't go around beatin' up on people, and I sure don't cut on 'em."

"Still," Hood said, "it would help me if you could tell me where you were when those assaults happened."

Andrew shook his head with disbelief, then asked for and was told the dates and time frames. "Home in bed, with the missus," he answered, "where I oughta be. Ask her if you don't believe me."

"Thanks," Hood said. He arose, walked to the door, then stopped and turned. "You know, Jacob's daughter, Angela, thinks someone might be watching her from behind her house."

"What are you sayin'?"

"Just wondering if you have any idea who it might be," Hood said.

"You think it was me wanderin' around behind her house?" Andrew asked, his tone combative. "Fuck, Francis. She's my niece."

"Not to spy on her," Hood said. "To protect her."

"From what?"

Hood realized his meeting with Andrew had descended from unproductive to confrontational. He regretted coming and was eager to leave. "I gotta go," he said.

"Hey, Francis," Andrew said as the sheriff arose from his chair. "Don't let that door hit you in the ass on your way out."

CHAPTER

16

Hood dipped the bristles into the paint, Pale Bluebell, and trimmed along the top of a window frame.

Linda was coming over. She had called and asked if he would be home.

He decided to begin the painting project that had been on his to-do list for months before he started recovery. He had promised to paint the living room if she would choose the color and buy the paint.

Although she had done her part months ago, the project had languished. Hood knew why. Drinking had taken priority—when he had free time and often when he didn't.

He had mixed feelings about starting now, when she couldn't help but notice. Matthew had told Hood he would know when he was making *real* progress because he would do things for other people without their knowledge.

As he applied another brush stroke, he acknowledged his action might not meet Matthew's definition of real progress, but it was progress.

Hood examined the strip of Pale Bluebell above the

window frame and smiled self-deprecatingly at the gulf that separated his abilities from Angela's artistry. He wiped the frame with a rag as he saw motion through the window and watched Linda's van stop at the curb.

He placed the brush on the paint can, climbed down the ladder, and opened the door for her.

She stepped inside, noticed the paint-spattered rag he held, and peered into the living room. "I like that color even more than I thought I would," she said. "Thanks for doing this."

"Sure," Hood said, distracted by the weight in her tone. "You want to sit down?"

"I can't stay," she said.

The phrase seemed momentous, not apologetic. Hood braced himself for words he didn't want to hear. "What's up?"

"They found a lump, Francis."

Hood stepped forward—an impulse—and embraced her. Although she hadn't been specific, he knew who "they" were and where the lump was "found." And he felt relieved, even as he berated himself that her awful news wasn't the awful news he dreaded. "When?"

"I found out yesterday. I went in for a routine mammogram." She expelled a short, staccato laugh. "Routine, right?"

Hood clung to her, as if they would prevent each other from collapsing where they stood.

"Anyway," she continued, "they took a biopsy. They say it's probably benign, but they need to be sure. I should know the results in a day or two."

Hood heard the unsteadiness in her voice.

"I wasn't going to tell you. I didn't want to worry you. I didn't want to put this burden on you. Certainly, not now. I was going to wait until I knew for sure but—" She struggled to remain composed.

He held her more tightly, hoping the pressure could vanquish her fears. "No," he said. "I'm glad you told me. We're in this together."

Hood felt her body convulse and shake as the sobs began, haltingly at first, then coming in steady waves.

Hours after Linda had gone, Hood dipped the roller into the tray and painted the recommended W pattern on the plaster wall.

His motions were automatic. His mind fixated on Linda's news, posed questions, imagined scenarios. The obsession triggered a desire to seek relief, and he knew his default solution all too well.

He knew he should call Matthew. He knew this was a situation where he was advised to seek help. He knew the only obstacle to doing so was his ego.

Still, he didn't make the call.

He mechanically rolled more paint onto the wall.

His cell phone rang.

He wiped his hands on the rag and answered, "Hello, this is Francis."

"It's me, John."

Hood heard his deputy's vain attempt not to slur his words. "Where are you?"

"I—I need to talk to you."

The urgency in his deputy's tone was unmistakable. "Are you okay?" Hood asked.

"Yeah. No. Not really."

"Where are you?" Hood repeated.

"At home."

"What happened?"

"I got pulled over. I was about a block from home. A block. It was a city cop. He gave me a DWI."

The admission staggered Hood—a one-two punch to the brain and the gut.

"I was a block away. A fucking block. And I was oh-point-nine, just over the limit. Of all the shit luck, I—"

"Stop," Hood shouted into the receiver.

The phone line was momentarily silent. "Stop what?" Young John asked.

"Stop making excuses."

"I'm not. It was a fluke. It was just bad luck."

"Listen to yourself," Hood said, his tone commanding. "You broke the law. You were drinking and driving. It doesn't matter if you were a block from home or just over the limit."

A silence ensued.

"I thought maybe you'd understand, I—"

"I do understand. You're in denial."

"I can't stop," Young John blurted. "Once I start, I can't stop. I've tried. I can't do it."

"Then you need help."

Hood heard his deputy choking back inevitable weeping. "I guess I should just resign."

"Unacceptable," Hood said.

"Why?"

"Because there's a solution. You have an addiction, John. You have a disease. If you're willing to face the consequences of your addiction, you can get well. If you're willing, I'll work with you."

"I'll try."

"Not good enough. I have to know that you're willing to get well. Yes or no."

"Yes."

"It's like everything's going to hell in a hand-basket right now," Hood said to Matthew.

"Everything?" Matthew said. They were seated across from each other in what had become their customary booth at Maggie's Diner. The interior was warm and bright; outside, a steady rain was punctuated by rumbles of thunder and flashes of lightning splitting the darkness.

Hood knew the question was Matthew's method of challenging exaggeration. "Well, some big things, at least."

"For example?"

"You know that deputy I was telling you about?" Hood asked. "Well, I reinstated him—I didn't tell him about my problem, by the way—but I ended up suspending him again, and he got a DWI."

"And?" Matthew prompted.

"And part of me feels like it's my fault. I mean, if I had confided in him or tried to work with him, if I hadn't suspended him for a second time, maybe—"

"Francis," Matthew interrupted, "I used to think I had that kind of power—if I did this, the other person would be fine, or if I hadn't done that, the other person wouldn't have messed up. I finally came to realize I don't control the universe, and I certainly can't control other people's behavior. The bottom line is I can't get anybody else drunk, and I can't get anybody else sober."

"You're saying I shouldn't be so hard on myself?"

"I'm saying you shouldn't think of yourself as God."

Hood was silent, but surprised he wasn't angry or resentful. "Guess I've still got a ways to go when it comes to humility," he said.

"You're not alone," Matthew said, his tone assuring.

"But that's not the worst of it. My wife may have breast cancer."

Matthew listened attentively while the sheriff described the situation. When Hood was finished, Matthew said, "I'm sorry. For me, uncertainty is the foundation of my greatest fears. Right now, you're awaiting results, potentially life-changing results. And you, and your wife, can't do anything to change those results. I know how I react; I always assume the worst. I try not to, but I do."

"So what do you do?"

"I try not to let it crush me. I try to have faith that everything will turn out all right, but the truth is I have doubts." Matthew paused. "This is a tough one, Francis, but you're not alone."

"I feel alone. And sometimes I feel like—regardless of what happens with the biopsy—she's never coming back. And then I hate myself for making this about me instead of about her."

"I know I've said this before, and I know you probably don't want to hear this right now, but you can only change yourself—your behaviors, your attitude. You can't decide what your deputy or your wife do, but you can change yourself in a way that might influence both their decisions and your reactions."

Hood was one of a foursome in the interrogation room. With him were Prosecutor Leo Pancrazio, defense attorney Only Ray Mosley, and his client Jet.

The preliminaries of the plea bargaining agreement had been hammered out. Through his public defender, Jet informed authorities he could provide information that would solve what he called "those church robberies."

In exchange, the prosecution would file a lesser charge of armed criminal action and, more importantly, assure administrative segregation during incarceration. Jet was not looking forward to solitary confinement, but it was preferable to what the Street Kings might do.

The details of the agreement—including recommended punishment—would depend on the value of what Jet divulged.

Leo, Hood knew, would endure public criticism for making a deal with someone who shot a law enforcement officer. But Hood also knew Leo rarely defended his actions publicly, not because he was arrogant or disdainful, but because he believed his job was to make, not justify, decisions.

Hood tried to focus, but Linda's revelation—*They found a lump*—echoed in his mind.

"Okay," Only Ray said to Jet. "Tell them what you know."

"Those church robberies," Jet said. "Me and another guy did those."

Hood was prepared. "These?" Hood asked. He read from a document that listed Holy Family Catholic Church Trivia Night and St. Michael's Catholic Church Sale-A-Rama, then slid the document to Only Ray, who shared it with Jet.

"Yeah, these two," Jet said.

"Any others?" Hood asked.

Jet shook his head.

They found a lump. Hood forced himself back to the moment. "Who's the other guy?"

Jet hesitated. "Just so you know, I'm not a rat. But me and this guy had a falling out. I mean, he stashed me in this roach-infested old building with no heat or water—"

"Name?" Hood had heard variations of the I'm- not-a-squealer-but rationalizations in the past. Criminals might weigh the question—do I do right for my partner, or do what's best for me?—but, ultimately, they'd find a way to justify their own self-interest. Hood waited.

"Randy. Randy Knaebel."

The name echoed in Hood's mind. "Wears a mitten?"

Everyone focused on the sheriff, obviously curious about how he knew.

"Yeah," Jet answered. "His right hand's fucked up."

They found a lump. The phrase bedeviled Hood. "Where do I find him?"

"We shared a place on Peavey Street, but he kicked me out. Told me I needed to lay low."

"Address?"

"Two thirty-one. Apartment B. It's a four-plex."

Hood wrote it down, arose from his chair, and left, nearly colliding with Maggie in the hallway.

"I was just coming to get you," she said. "I figured you'd want to know right away. They just took Jacob Grace to the hospital."

Hood screwed his mouth into a quizzical frown. "What happened?"

"Someone cut his throat."

CHAPTER

17

As he drove to the scene of the latest assault on Jacob Grace, Hood recalled the advice, "Wherever you are, be there."

He needed to stay in the moment. He couldn't get Linda's phrase—*They found a lump*—out of his head, despite telling himself repeatedly he couldn't do anything about that. Still, the obsessive thought, like an addiction, crept into every aspect of his day.

As Hood rounded a bend on Old Cedar Creek Road, he saw Wally standing at the roadside. Hood slowed and parked on the shoulder behind Wally's cruiser, which was nose to nose with a late-model SUV.

Be here, Hood reminded himself, even as he shifted his attention and radioed Art, another of his veteran deputies. He instructed Art to stake out Randy Knaebel's apartment, then provided the Peavey Street address and a suspect description, including the mittened right hand.

Exiting his cruiser, he approached Wally and asked, "What've we got?"

"Ambulance already took Jacob to the hospital, but those

are the people," Wally said, gesturing to an elderly couple standing beside the SUV, "who heard the screams, stopped, and called it in."

Hood approached the couple. "I'm your sheriff, Francis Hood," he said.

"Ross Radamacher," the man said. He extended his hand. "And this is my wife, Julie."

Hood shook each of their hands in turn. "I understand you made the 9-1-1 call."

"We did," Ross said. "We were driving home—we've been out antiquing all morning—and we heard screams."

"Loud screams," Julie added.

"They were loud, all right," Ross affirmed.

Be here, Hood told himself. Be here and be patient, but patience eluded him. He was eager to see the crime scene, the skies were overcast and threatening rain, and he was expecting a call from Art.

"So I stopped the car," Ross said. "And I got out and heard the screams coming from that direction." He pointed across the road to a rutted farm lane beside a fenced field. "And I heard a motor running, like a mower, but that was farther away. I didn't know whether to walk down there or not. I mean, I didn't know—"

Hood's cell rang. He answered Art's call, asked him to "hang on," then said to the Radamachers, "Give Wally your contact information. We'll be in touch if we need anything."

"Already did," Ross said. "Does that mean we can go?"

Hood waved dismissively, walked back to his cruiser and

said, "Go ahead, Art."

"I'm parked near Randy's place. No sign of him. What do you want me to do?"

"Just sit tight for now, but keep me posted."

He ended the call, rejoined Wally, and, together, they crossed the road and started along the lane.

They found a lump. Incapable of eliminating the phrase from his mind, Hood surrendered to its echo.

"It's not far," Wally said. "When I arrived, the ambulance was already parked up the lane. You could see the lights from the road. And the old couple was right. I heard a motor in the distance, sounded like a chain saw. Once I got to about where we are now, I could see the EMTs tending to a guy sitting on the ground, so I ran up there. As I got closer, I saw it was Jacob Grace. His neck and forehead were zip-tied to the fence post. His hands were, too; they were zip-tied behind his back. And his throat was cut, and blood covered his chin and had soaked through the front of his shirt. The EMTs said they needed to cut the zip ties, so I went ahead and did it and collected them as evidence."

"Good," Hood said.

Wally stopped walking. "This is it." He pointed to where a new fence post had been placed in the ground. "Jacob was over there. I figured he must've been replacing some fence, because there's a post-hole digger, some posts, and spools of barbed wire right over there."

"Hutch is letting him stay in his stable," Hood said, "in exchange for some work around the place. Speaking of Hutch, has he been around?"

"Not so far as I know."

"I'm gonna call him," Hood said. His call was sent to voice mail, and he left a message for Hutch to return his call.

Hood scanned the area and noted a portable radio and battered toolbox with a metal bottle perched upright on the lid. Hood put on a plastic glove, unscrewed the bottle top, and smelled the contents. "That's not water," he said.

"Booze?" Wally asked.

"Whiskey," Hood said. When his cell phone rang, he answered Art's call.

"A beat-up Oldsmobile just pulled up in front," Art said, "and a guy matching your suspect description went inside."

"On my way," Hood said. He turned to Wally. "Give this area a good going over. Call the crime lab—ask for Sandra, if she's available—if you come across anything that could be evidence." He looked skyward. "Oh, and hope this gully-washer holds off for a while."

"Anything?" Hood asked Art, as he joined his deputy outside Randy Knaebel's apartment.

"Not since he went in," Art answered. "How do you want to do this?"

The strategy was simple. Art watched the side window while Hood knocked on the door.

"Who is it?" Randy's voice asked from within.

"It's your sheriff, Francis Hood."

"What d'ya want?"

SENSE OF GRACE

"We met at Angela Grace's house. I just want to talk to you."

"About what?"

"I just have a few questions."

"Gimme a minute, okay?"

Hood heard footsteps receding. He scurried to the corner of the house and signaled Art. When the window was opened and a leg protruded, Art pulled Randy through and pinned him to the ground.

"Hello, Randy," Hood said as he approached.

"What's this all about," Randy said, spitting a fallen piece of leaf from his mouth.

"You're under arrest."

"For what?"

Hood removed the sheet of paper he had read earlier to Jet, unfolded it, and listed the robberies.

"I had nothin' to do with them," Randy protested.

"Just decided to leave by the window, huh?"

"I got nothin' to say."

"Good, because I've got other places to be," Hood said. "Art will read you your rights."

Hood's other place to be—Huhman County Hospital— was largely unproductive.

He learned Jacob Grace's throat had been lacerated by a serrated blade—according to the ER doctor's evaluation of the wound—but the wound was neither deep nor life threatening.

He learned even less during a brief visit with Jacob, who was suffering, seething, and silent. The neck wound had been

199

bandaged, and Hood observed the forehead and wrist abrasions where the man had struggled against the zip ties.

Hood was driving back to the crime scene when Hutch returned his call.

"Was Jacob putting in some new fence for you today?" the sheriff asked.

"What do you mean, was? He's s'posed to call me when he's done."

"Yeah, well, can you meet me out at that fence row?"

"Where I dropped him off?"

"Yeah," Hood said. "I'm just about there."

"I guess. What's up?"

"Just meet me. Okay?"

"Okay."

Hood rejoined Wally, and the two lawmen waited and watched until Hutch's pickup navigated the rutted lane and stopped.

"What's goin' on," Hutch asked through the open driver's side window. "Where's Jacob?"

"In the hospital," Hood said. "He got assaulted again."

"Try to do the right thing," Hutch mumbled. He got out of the truck. "I guess this just ain't workin' out."

"What's not working out?" Hood asked.

"He's s'posed to be helpin' around here," Hutch answered. "Not gettin' drunk and gettin' himself hacked up all the time."

"What makes you think he was drunk?"

"He's always drunk." Hutch shook his head in disbelief as he studied the fencerow. "Look there," he continued. "He's been out here most of the day and he got—what?—maybe four new posts in."

"What time did you bring him out here?"

"I don't know," Hutch said. "I took him to his doctor's appointment this morning, and when we got back, we loaded up those posts and wire over there, and I brought him out here."

"Dr. Daniels?" Hood asked.

"Yeah."

"What time was that?"

"Eight forty-five. Had to wait. Took about an hour."

"What were you doing after you brought Jacob out here?"

"Sawin' up a downed tree behind the house."

Hood recalled mention of the distant sound of a motor. "The whole time?"

"Mostly. Between cuttin' and haulin' and stackin' and—" He paused. "Wait a minute. Are you wonderin' if I done it? 'Cause that ain't right, sheriff." Hutch flung his arms skyward, let them drop. "That ain't right, 'cause I done the Christian thing. I'm the guy—the only guy—who took 'im in. I did what's right and you're accusin' me. I don't—"

"I'm not accusing you," Hood said. "I'm just trying to establish—"

"I'll let God be my judge," Hutch said. He climbed into the cab and started the truck. "It's just like the Gospels tell me," he called through the window. "I may be persecuted on earth for the same good deeds that earn rewards in heaven."

He drove away.

CHAPTER
18

Hood was encouraged.

Again he had made an appointment and again had been invited into Angela's kitchen, a gesture that seemed much less formal than their initial meeting in her parlor. This time, fresh coffee had been brewed, obviously for him.

He was less pleased with the purpose of his visit. Delivering news about an attack on Angela's father had become repetitive, almost mundane, and this time he also intended to inform her of the arrest of her childhood friend Randy Knaebel.

"So," Angela said, placing her teacup on the kitchen table and sitting perpendicular to Hood, "any luck finding out who's been watching me?"

"No." Hood looked at her eyes, at her veil, and at Prince, who sat at her side, ever alert. "There was no DNA on the toothpick we found in the woods. The toothpick Randy gave me is the same brand, but that could mean any number of things— he accidentally dropped it, someone's trying to implicate him, or it's just coincidence."

Angela nodded.

"I'm here," Hood added, "because I wanted you to know I arrested your friend, Randy, on another matter."

"Really?" she said. "For what?"

"A pair of robberies."

She stared into her teacup, said nothing.

"You don't seem entirely surprised," Hood ventured.

She looked toward him. "I am, and I'm not. Ethan took it upon himself to run a background check on him, and he told me Randy had a record—trespassing and theft, or something. I mean, until the other day, I hadn't seen him since grade school, but I've been getting this vibe that he's hiding something. He seems, well," she searched for the right word, "different. That's the only way I can describe it."

"Different how?"

"I don't know. Ever since we were kids, Randy had a chip on his shoulder. It was like his deformity gave him an excuse to be mad at the world. I think he enjoyed playing the victim role. He was always asking other people to do things for him, things he could do himself. Sometimes our moms would bring us to the same park, and we'd chase the geese or play on the playground and he'd want me to start the merry-go-round or push him on the swings. Of course, that all stopped after this—" she said, pointing to her veil, then continued, "After my mom and brothers were killed, it was a while before I went back to school. Randy was the first kid—the only kid, really—who came up to me and said he was sorry about my family and what happened to me. He even gave me a present; he said it was to help cheer me up. It was a snow-globe village, not one of the big ones, but a little one. I think I knew even then that he stole it, but it didn't matter."

Hood's thoughts shifted to the Sale-A-Rama robbery.

"We became friends," Angela continued, "I'm sure the counselors I saw back then have some name for it—like visibly-deformed-kids-bonding-against-the-cruel-world syndrome—but for us, it just seemed normal.

"And then, one day, he wasn't in school, and I found out his mother had taken him and moved away. Not long after that, my guardians moved me to a different school, too, and I didn't see Randy for years until he turned up the other day at my fundraiser. I was—"

"Your fundraiser?" Hood interrupted.

"Yes. I host a pancake breakfast fundraiser each year for Helping Children Through Art." She noticed the change in the sheriff's expression as she spoke. "What?" she said.

"Where was your fundraiser?"

"St. Aloysius school. Why?"

"Which adjoins the church, right?"

"Yes. Why?"

"The robberies," Hood answered.

"What about them?"

"They occurred at fundraisers at churches."

Angela sat back in her chair. Her eyes widened as the connection registered. "You don't—" she began, then paused, "you don't think he was planning to rob my fundraiser?"

Hood hesitated, "I guess we'll never know."

Angela shook her head. "That's just too—I don't even know."

They sat silently for several moments before Hood said, "There's something else."

"What?" Angela scrutinized the sheriff's expression. "Is it about my father?"

Hood nodded. "He's in the hospital. He was assaulted again."

She closed her eyes, then asked, "What happened this time?"

"He was tied to a fence post in broad daylight. His throat was cut—not too deep, but not superficial either."

Angela sighed, a response that seemed rooted more in frustration than surprise or horror.

"More coffee?" she asked.

Before Hood could respond, she stood, carried his cup to the counter and began refilling it—all under Prince's watchful eyes.

"You seem—" Hood began, struggling for a word or phrase to describe her reaction.

"Unmoved?" she volunteered when the pause persisted. "I don't know, sheriff. I don't know what I am. It's not that I hate my father. At least I don't want to hate him. I just don't want him taking up time in my head, and that's what's happened since he got out and these assaults began."

She placed his cup on the table. "I thought I'd come to terms with all this," she continued, sweeping a hand in the air. "Some victims find a cause; they lobby lawmakers, advocate change, raise money to cure diseases. I never had that passion.

I had art."

"What about your art classes, the Reaching Kids group?"

"I don't know if that was a passion so much as an extension of my art." She sat. "At one time I enjoyed some popularity and the wealth that came with it. I had the resources to create the school, and it was something I wanted to do."

"You said 'had.'"

"Fame is fleeting in the art world," Angela said. "I'm not as rich as people think I am. Don't get me wrong; I'm not poor. I saved wisely and I set money aside for the school—which I believe in—and I still do all right, but it's nothing like it was."

"Can I ask you a personal question?"

"I thought these were all personal questions," she said, with no suggestion of judgment or hesitancy.

"Why do you still live here?"

"This is my home."

"But, I mean, after what happened here. After your career took off and you had all those opportunities to—"

"Leave," Angela said, completing the sentence. "Leave what? I can't leave me behind, and I can't leave my past behind. I wake up each morning and look in the mirror, and there I am. It doesn't matter if the mirror is in New York or Los Angeles or Huhman County."

"I'm sorry," Hood said. "I shouldn't—"

"And," she interrupted, "do you know what I see? Sometimes I see a woman who has done all right for herself, an artist who creates challenging images, who nurtures young artists, who has found meaning and purpose." Angela again arose from her seat, prompting Prince to stand. Hood sensed the shepherd bristle with unease, tension. "Sometimes I see a lost little girl who never got the chance to know her family. And sometimes I just see a monster, a horribly disfigured monster."

She walked quietly and purposely out of the kitchen. Prince trotted beside her, obviously troubled by her demeanor.

Hood sat stunned. He swiveled his head and looked at the doorway, then scanned the vacant room. He felt somehow too paralyzed even to reach for the coffee cup. He waited, wordlessly, wondering what he could have said or should have said. After what seemed a long time, Odessa came in and told him Angela would not return. Hood nodded as if he already knew, as if he had lingered only in anticipation of Odessa showing him out.

Hood sat at his desk, leafed through the documents in his inbox and thought about Linda.

They found a lump, Francis.

He wanted to call her, but something was holding him back. Examine your motives was among the suggestions repeated by his peers in recovery.

His motive was to find out the results of the biopsy. Or was it?

He knew Linda. He certainly knew her well enough to know she would call him as soon as she found out. After all, she had told him about the lump, even though she said she didn't want to worry him.

Was his desire to call sparked by the more selfish motive of letting her know he was thinking about her?

So what if it was? He was thinking about her. Why shouldn't he? He did care. He cared about her and about their future together. It wasn't some passing thought; it was ever present.

He called, got her voice mail, and left a message asking her to return his call.

He disconnected, moved the stack of papers from the inbox to the desktop, and stared vacantly at the documents. The top report outlined an early morning break-in at A-One Auto Parts.

Wherever you are, be there.

He imagined himself at the scene, standing in the darkened delivery area at the rear of the auto parts store, prying open a rear door, triggering an alarm, fleeing empty-handed before hearing approaching sirens.

Next was a jail intake form for Randy Knaebel, completed with trademark thoroughness by the department's jail supervisor Fred Schell. Attached were the obligatory mug shots and copies of Randy's Missouri driver's license and criminal record.

Hood scanned the form. He noted date of birth and calculated Randy was 37, the same as Angela. The line for parents' name listed his mother Julie Knaebel, deceased. The driver's license was valid.

He flipped to the criminal history and was surprised by its

brevity. Randy had only two prior convictions in Missouri—a misdemeanor trespassing and a felony stealing. Both had occurred two years ago in St. Louis.

Hood sensed something was missing. During his tenure with the department, Hood had learned that when standard databases were inadequate, a fount of institutional knowledge was available to him.

He carried the forms to the dispatch station and placed the mug shots on Maggie's desk.

"Know this guy?" he asked.

She studied the photos and information. "No. Should I?"

"Name's Randy Knaebel. He didn't list both parents, just his mother, Julie Knaebel, deceased."

"I know some Knaebels, but I don't think I know a Julie."

"She was married to Randy's father, but she divorced him when Randy was a child, and she took back her maiden name. I'm trying to find out who Randy's father is."

"No idea."

"Okay," Hood said.

"Is it important?"

"I don't know."

"Want me to try to find out?"

"Please," Hood said.

INTERLUDE:
Amazing Grace

Angela is frustrated by her failures.

She needs more illustrations to fulfill her commission for the children's book. She is satisfied with the two she has completed but cannot understand her inability to translate "Amazing Grace" from sound to sketch.

Perhaps a different medium is necessary, so she purposely switches from colored pencil to acrylic paint.

She lowers the phonograph needle and the hymn begins.

Amazing grace!
How sweet the sound, that saved a wretch like me!
I once was lost, but now am found
Was blind, but now I see.

Sensations are aroused. She slashes bold strokes of cadmium yellow onto a canvas.

She is uncertain whether her synesthesia has been triggered by the notes and lyrics, or she is merely expressing her frustration, but she does not stop. She stabs the brush tip into warm white and adds a series of arcs.

'Twas grace that taught my heart to fear.
And grace my fears relieved;
How precious did that grace appear
The hour I first believed.

Angela fears what she is creating is artificial. The sensations are false; the image is fabricated. She suspects she might confess her fears to God, if she believed in God.

Through many dangers, toils and snares,
I have already come;
'Tis grace hath brought me safe thus far
And grace will lead me home.

She scrubs the tip of her brush in perylene red and smears a large "X" across the canvas. Another failure.

CHAPTER

19

"This is different," Ethan observed. "Usually I come to visit you. To what do I owe this"—he searched for the word—"courtesy?"

"Randy's been arrested," Angela said. She sat in the visitor's chair facing his massive desk. Today, she wore a mask, not a veil. Prince sat beside the chair, alert to the unfamiliar surroundings. "I need a lawyer to defend him."

Ethan pushed his chair from his desk and leaned back, unable to mask his smug expression. "I haven't done a criminal case in—"

"Not you," she interrupted. "You don't even like Randy. I'm asking you for a reference."

"Dan Haslag does almost all our criminal work. He's really good. Want me to see if he's available to join us?"

"Not now," Angela said. "I'll make an appointment."

Ethan leaned forward, folded his hands on the desktop. "What makes you say I don't like Randy? I hardly even know the guy."

"You did a background check on him."

"He was spying on you."

The accusation hit Angela like a slap in the face. She hesitated a moment, unsure if she had heard him correctly. "He what?"

"He was spying on you—from behind your house. How did he explain the toothpick you found?"

Angela eyed him warily. "How did you know about the toothpick?"

"You told me."

"I didn't."

Angela knew in that instant that Ethan realized his mistake.

"You must have forgotten," he insisted. "Or maybe it was the sheriff who mentioned it. I don't know."

Angela had no reason to believe the sheriff would have done so, but she resolved to ask him before pursuing the matter with Ethan. "I need to go."

"Angela Grace is on the phone," Maggie told her boss.

Hood wasn't expecting her call. He had heard Angela had posted Randy's Knaebel's bond and was seeking private counsel to represent him. He was both clueless and curious about the nature of her call. "Put her through," he told Maggie. When the connection was made, he said, "This is your sheriff."

"It's Angela."

"Hello."

"Sorry to bother you, but I just had this baffling conversation with Ethan Diffenbaugh. He's my attorney. You met him."

"Yes."

"Well, I asked him to refer me to a criminal attorney for Randy, and he did, but he also accused Randy of spying on me and mentioned the toothpick you found behind my house."

Hood waited, expecting her to continue.

"Did you mention the toothpick to him?"

"No," Hood said. "No way would I have discussed possible evidence with him."

"That's what I thought," Angela said. "So how did he know?"

"Did you ask him?"

"He said one of us mentioned it, but I know I didn't. That's why I called you." Angela paused, then added, "Ethan had this look, like he realized he'd screwed up and said too much."

"You know him much better than I do."

"I don't trust Ethan anymore. His attitude borders on jealousy. I'm not going to hire the attorney he recommended for Randy. For some reason, Ethan's got it in for Randy. Did I tell you he ran a background check?"

"Yes," Hood answered.

"I thought so."

Hood wondered, silently, if Ethan had gone even further.

It was Angela, however, who voiced his thoughts when she said, "I wouldn't be entirely surprised if Ethan planted that toothpick just to turn me against Randy."

SENSE OF GRACE

* * * * *

When Hood was chief deputy, nearly a decade earlier, his fellow officers referred to the Huhman County Circuit Court as the halls of injustice. That characterization faded as newly elected judges and prosecutors gradually lifted the veil of mystery that once shrouded the workings of the court and began communicating more openly among themselves and with law enforcement and the public.

Hood climbed the wide stone steps from his basement office to the expansive second-floor hallway outside the cavernous Division II courtroom. A crowd—defendants, attorneys, family members—had gathered for the twice-monthly Law Day session, held on the first and third Tuesdays of each month to conduct criminal proceedings, including arraignments, trial settings, and some dispositions.

Hood spotted Randy Knaebel standing in a corner, conferring with a woman wearing a blue, pin-striped skirt and jacket, and holding a briefcase. Hood had seen the woman in the courthouse and knew she was an attorney but couldn't recall her name. Randy had made an obvious effort to appear presentable. He was clean-shaven, and his hair had been cut. He wore a powder-blue, long-sleeved shirt, a striped tie, and navy slacks. Although his black shoes had been polished, the rounded heels and creased leather betrayed wear.

When two bailiffs opened the doors to the courtroom, Hood stood beside the hallway sign—"Quiet Please"—and watched people funnel into the two aisles separating the center seating from two side sections.

Angela was not among the group.

Hood entered last. He noticed the majority of people had gathered near the front, presumably to avoid delays as the cases were called. He had his choice of empty seats in the rear and chose a center section, back row, aisle seat that offered a sweeping vantage point.

"Huhman County Circuit Court, Division II, is now in session. The honorable Joyce Patrick presiding," the bailiff announced, silencing the buzz of conversation as the judge ascended to the bench.

The first two cases, both trial settings, were quickly dispatched, and the judge was hearing a request to reduce bond when Hood noticed movement in the periphery of his vision. He glanced toward the aisle to his right and saw Angela Grace, accompanied by Prince, walk several rows ahead and seat herself in a side gallery aisle seat. She wore a flexible plastic mask instead of a veil and did not seem to notice his presence. Or, if she did, she did not acknowledge him.

Hood shifted his attention from Angela, to Randy, to the proceedings. His repetitive pattern continued until he noticed Angela's sidelong glance to the opposite aisle. The sheriff followed her gaze and caught a glimpse of Dr. Steven Daniels until he sat and disappeared from view. Hood's curiosity was piqued momentarily before his attention was shifted abruptly by the bailiff's announcement of "Case 2312, State vs. Randy Scott Knaebel."

Randy and his attorney approached the defendant's table

and remained standing while Judge Patrick read the two robbery charges filed against him. "Do you understand the charges against you?" she asked.

"Yes, your honor," Randy answered, with rehearsed respect.

"And how do you plead?"

His attorney leaned forward and answered, "My client pleads not guilty, your honor."

The judge asked Randy's attorney how much time she would need to prepare his defense and how long she envisioned a trial might last, based on an estimate of evidence and witnesses.

Hood was familiar with the drill. The trial setting was largely a formality in many criminal cases; most resulted in a plea agreement.

The judge suggested a trial date three months in the future, and the defense and prosecution agreed.

With the trial setting completed, Randy and his attorney retreated and exited the courtroom.

Hood watched as Angela and Prince moved into the aisle. She gave Hood a slight nod of acknowledgement as she and the shepherd passed him and left the courtroom. Within moments, Daniels also exited.

Hood did the same.

From his vantage point just outside the courtroom door, he watched Angela confer with Randy and his attorney in a corner near the top of the staircase. A distance away, the doctor lingered just outside the far courtroom door he had exited.

What, Hood wondered, was the physician's apparent

interest in Randy's case? His curiosity was interrupted when Randy looked up and noticed the doctor's presence. Randy spoke to his lawyer—in a whisper Hood could not decipher—and the attorney crossed the hallway and addressed Daniels, who hadn't moved.

Hood saw the conversation between the doctor and lawyer was animated but was unable to overhear their words. Daniels listened, looked first at Randy, then at Angela.

Their brief discussion ended with the lawyer returning to Angela and her client while the doctor walked in the opposite direction toward the elevator.

As Daniels waited, he began to whistle. Hood wasn't sure whether the action was involuntary or intentional, but he recognized the popular hymn, "Amazing Grace."

When the elevator door opened, the doctor disappeared inside.

Turning his attention back to the trio, Hood focused on Angela. Tremors shook her shoulders. A single convulsion coursed through her entire body, and her wide-eyed reaction revealed some bizarre blend of surprise and confusion. Prince tensed but seemed to await her command. Without a word to her companions, she turned and, with Prince at her side, fled down the staircase.

Baffled by the scene, Hood wondered, what the hell just happened?

INTERLUDE:

Amazing Grace (reprise)

The doctor's whistled melody of "Amazing Grace" reverberates in Angela's mind, triggering a succession of colors, lines, and shapes.

The tune from Daniels was unlike the version she recalled her mother singing and unlike the song on her record album. Consequently, the visual playing itself out in her mind is unlike her previous failed attempts to capture it on canvas.

Yet, somehow, it is strangely familiar.

She had raced down the courthouse steps, not to catch up with Daniels, but to rush home and attempt to paint the image frozen in her mind's eye. Her concentration remained so fixed, so focused, and so intense that the short drive home seemed both interminable and imaginary.

As she sits before the blank canvas, palette in hand, she flourishes her brush like a conductor's wand, synchronizing strokes of color with her memory of the doctor's rendition.

When the image begins to reveal itself, she knows she is capturing something true. As she paints, she drifts beyond consciousness, beyond self-channeling her synesthesia, memory, and creativity.

Angela is surprised when she regains awareness of her surroundings and sees darkness gathering beyond her windows. She knows only that hours have passed and the painting is complete.

She returns her focus to the image that eluded her earlier attempts.

And she recognizes it. She has seen it before.

Where? When?

She is unsure. All she knows is she saw it a long time ago.

She arises from her seat, climbs the stairs to the upper floor, and pulls the cord affixed to a hatch in the ceiling. She unfolds the ladder that leads to the attic, where she recently had retrieved her mother's album of hymns and record player. Angela had stored everything her mother had saved, including the artwork her daughter had created as a child.

CHAPTER

20

Hood had been rebuffed.

He reminded himself not to take it personally, but he did.

Puzzled by the scene at the courthouse, he had driven to Angela's house and knocked on the door.

As usual, Odessa answered.

He asked to see Angela.

"I'm sorry," Odessa had said. "She's not seeing visitors."

He argued he was on official business, but Odessa was adamant. She said Angela had given her "strict instructions" not to be disturbed.

Hood said he would return the next day. Then he drove away, hammering frustrations on the steering wheel as he returned to the sheriff's department.

When he entered, Maggie, who was on a call, hailed him with a wait-a-minute gesture.

He lingered at the dispatch station, resisting the temptation to pour himself some coffee that was too black to be fresh.

"Young John called," Maggie said when she ended her phone conversation. "He wondered if you were available. I told him you were in court, but should be back," she paused and looked at a clock, "about now."

Hood shrugged. "I suppose—"

"Good, because he's on his way."

"Okay," Hood said, his resignation apparent. "Send him back when he gets here." He walked to his office and was still standing behind his desk and distractedly shuffling phone messages when Young John appeared in his doorway.

"C'mon in," Hood said.

Young John entered, closed the door, and sat. Although he seemed eager to speak, he remained silent, his expression sheepish.

"What can I do for you?" Hood prompted.

"I got an attorney and asked her if there was anything I could do to show I'm serious about this DWI. She suggested I familiarize myself with recovery programs and with SATOP."

Hood was familiar with SATOP, the acronym for Missouri's Substance Abuse Traffic Offender Program, among the standard punishment options for first-time DWI offenders.

"So," Young John said, "I found this guy Matthew—he's a recovering alcoholic who pretty much runs SATOP—and we talked."

Mention of Matthew's name funneled Hood's scattered attention into complete focus. He listened intently as Young John continued.

"He had some ideas. He said there were inpatient and outpatient programs, as well as a bunch of recovery meetings. Some of them meet as often as twice a day, and they're free.

So I've been—" he paused. "I'm sorry, you look like you have something to say."

"No," Hood said. For the second time that day, he found himself attempting to process information he didn't comprehend. He wondered if Matthew had been aware Young John not only was a deputy, but was the same deputy Hood previously had discussed. He also wondered if Matthew's suggestions included the Recovery Rules meeting Hood attended. Although Young John hadn't specified, Hood contemplated the potential awkwardness if he and his deputy attended the same meeting.

"Well," Young John said. "I talked to my wife, and she thinks my drinking's gotten out of control, and—well, I hate to say it—she may be right. It's like, like flipping a switch. Once I have that first drink, I can't stop. That probably sounds weird to you."

"No," Hood said. "I understand." A part of him wanted to say more, but he didn't.

"So, I wanted to sound you out about taking some time off. I know I can take a leave of absence through the Family and Medical Leave Act, but I don't want to leave you short-handed. I mean, I could probably wait—"

"It's fine. We'll work it out. Your well-being is top priority."

"You're sure?"

Hood saw his deputy was on the threshold of tears. "Absolutely. I'm looking at a deputy with tremendous potential. That's the guy I want to work with."

Young John stood.

Hood followed, then did something he never had done before. He walked around his desk and hugged an employee.

"You are nothing if not punctual," Odessa remarked as she opened the front door to the sheriff.

"Is she here?" Hood asked.

"Of course. You made an appointment. She's expecting you."

Hood followed Odessa inside and was surprised when he was led past the parlor and the kitchen and into Angela's studio.

Odessa announced the sheriff and withdrew, leaving Hood to scan the interior. Angela, who was perched on a stool in the center of the room, turned to face him, shifting her view away from two easels, each displaying an artwork. The images were remarkably similar, but one obviously was the work of a more mature artist.

Angela wore a paint-spattered apron over blue jeans and a tan turtleneck sweater. Her long, daffodil blonde hair was tied in a ponytail, and a dark veil, not a mask, hid the lower portion of her face.

Prince sat at the foot of a nearby work table strewn with an array of brushes, paints, a palette knife, and other art supplies unfamiliar to Hood. Paintings and drawings in various stages of completion were displayed on shelves or arranged—sometimes three deep—leaning against the interior wall.

"Please, come in," Angela said to the sheriff, who had

paused just inside the room.

"Thanks for seeing me." He stepped forward into the warmth and natural light permeating the room. "I came by yesterday after the court—"

"Sorry. I was working." She gestured to the painting on the easel nearer her, and added, "on this."

Hood concentrated on the painting. He tried to interpret how the colors and shapes affected him. Since he had met Angela, he found himself becoming more attuned to the sights and sounds of his everyday life. The painting, however, inspired nothing. He had no reaction, no thoughts, no feelings. He was simply baffled. "I don't understand."

"I painted it when I came home," Angela said. "Now, look at the other one."

Hood shifted his gaze to the easel holding a similar, but much less accomplished, artwork. His exposure to art was limited, but he was pretty sure he was looking at a child's creation.

"I painted that one when I was seven," Angela said. "I put the date on the back."

Hood faced her. "I'm confused."

"So am I," she said. "I knew when I was painting yesterday that I was recreating an image I had painted before. When I finished, I went to the attic—my mom saved everything—and found the one I painted about thirty years ago."

Hood hesitated a beat. "Now I'm really confused."

"Both were triggered by the same sensation." Angela said. "That's how it happens sometimes with my synesthesia.

I hear something, and shapes and colors spill like an avalanche into my mind. That's what happened yesterday, and I had to paint it as quickly as I could. But it wasn't just the same song, it was the same notes, tempo, and phrasing I painted when I was a child."

"How can you be sure?" Hood asked. "If it's been thirty years—"

"Because it's a song I've been trying to paint lately. I got out an album of hymns my mother used to sing to me, and I've been painting the sensations from some of the songs, but I've failed every time I've tried to paint 'Amazing Grace.' See that group of paintings stacked against the wall over there?" She pointed to the canvases. "Those are the rejects."

"'Amazing Grace,'" Hood repeated. "That's what Daniels was whistling yesterday outside the courtroom. What was he doing there, anyway?"

"I guess he wanted to see what would happen to his son."

"His son," Hood repeated, staggered by the revelation. "Dr. Daniels is Randy's father?"

"Yes. I thought you knew," Angela said. "They're estranged. They haven't spoken to each other since Randy came back here, since he was a child, in fact."

"But if the new painting duplicates something you created thirty years ago, and they're both based on the same song, that means you must have heard—"

"Exactly," she said. "I heard Dr. Daniels's version of 'Amazing Grace' when I was a child."

"There must be an explanation," Hood said. "Maybe your

parents took you to him for an ear infection or something, and you just don't remember. Maybe he, instead of his wife, brought Randy to the playground one time. Or maybe you had a play date at their home. There are any number of possible circumstances."

"I thought the same thing," Angela said. "I even remember my mother was one of his patients, and I went to his office with her once or twice, but that's not it. No, I distinctly remember painting that picture in my bedroom upstairs. And I remember Dr. Daniels being here—not in my room, but in this house—when I was a kid."

"Still," Hood said, "maybe he was making a house call. Maybe he was a friend of the family. He's your father's doctor now."

"He's what?"

"He's been treating your father—for the ear and the other attacks. But you said you remember the tune from when you were a child. Did this all happen before the—?"

"The massacre," she said, completing his question. "Yes. About a year before that."

Hood stood quietly, frustrated and exasperated because he had no solution to offer. He looked at Angela. Although her expression was hidden by the veil, her eyes signaled she was troubled. "What are you thinking?" he asked.

"I think I need some time to process this," she said.

CHAPTER
21

Randy made no attempt to hide his surprise when he answered the knock, opened his front door, and faced Angela.

"May we come in?" she asked, nodding to Prince, who accompanied her.

"Of course."

The room they entered was sparsely furnished. An oval coffee table, its lacquer checkered, was positioned within reach of a tattered sofa and matching chair, likely purchased from a thrift store.

"I know it's not much," Randy said, reacting to her appraisal of the room. "I don't get a lot of visitors." He offered a self-deprecating laugh. "Have a seat. Can I get you something to drink? I have beer, water—" He stopped himself, unable to think of other choices.

"Nothing for me, thanks," Angela said. She sat in the chair as Prince sat beside her.

"I, um, if this is about paying the bond or the lawyer, I'm really grateful, as I said, but I'm—"

"It's not about that."

"Okay?" He sat on an edge of a sofa cushion.

"Did you spy on me from behind my house?"

"Spy on you?" he asked, his tone incredulous. "No—of course not. Why would I do that?"

Angela had no doubt he was telling the truth. "Never mind."

"No," he protested. "I want to know why you would think that."

"I saw movement back there, and a toothpick was found. Someone suggested it might be you."

"Who?"

"It doesn't matter."

"It does to me," Randy said.

"I believe you when you say it wasn't you. I don't want to name names, so can we just drop it?"

Randy knew she would not relent. "Okay," he conceded.

"Tell me about your father," she said.

"What about him?" Randy asked. "Until he showed up at the courthouse the other day—which I had nothin' to do with, by the way—I hadn't seen him for almost thirty years, since my mother left him and took me with her."

"Do you know the circumstances—why she left, I mean?"

"From what little I remember, their marriage was a train wreck waiting to happen. After it did, I do remember my mom—I overheard her talking to her sisters or cousins—refer to my dad as a 'philandering louse.'"

"So your mom thought he was cheating on her?"

"I don't know if she knew or just suspected."

"Did your mom ever say who she thought he was cheating with?"

"Not that I recall but what did I know? I was, like, eight."

"Is that why you don't talk to your father? Because your mom—"

"Why would I talk to him?"

"Because he's your father."

"Do you talk to your father?" Randy challenged, immediately wishing he could take back the words he'd blurted.

Angela hesitated. "You're right," she said, a chastised whisper.

"I didn't mean," Randy began, leaning forward. "What I meant was, when kids grow up, their relationship with their parents can be, I don't know, difficult. I get that. After what your father did to you, you have every right to keep your distance. In my case, it wasn't what my father did; it was what he didn't do. He never gave me his attention or time. I never felt that he loved me. I always felt like a disappointment to him because of this." He removed the mitten and showed her the withered, deformed claw-like appendage that was his right hand. "My father was a doctor and his father was a doctor and his father's father, and he knew from the day I was born that I was never going to carry on the—"

Randy stopped, choking back a combination of rage and pain.

Angela remained still. Prince tilted his head and cocked his ears, as if trying to understand.

"I hate him," Randy said, his tone casual. "I hate him, and

I hate myself for hating him. Does that make sense? I hate him because every time I see him, I see disappointment in his eyes, disappointment about me."

"You couldn't help that," Angela said.

"Don't," Randy said. "I've disappointed everyone." He looked away. "And now I've disappointed you."

"You haven't—"

Randy held up his right hand in a halting gesture, cutting her off in mid-sentence.

"I think I should go," Angela said. She stood. Prince followed. Together, they left quietly.

Hood sat at his desk, but his focus was elsewhere.

He wanted to be at a recovery meeting, but Matthew's weekly session was two days away. He began to appreciate what a person meant by the phrase, "I need a meeting."

His thoughts drifted to Young John. Hood wondered if he had done "the right thing," a phrase repeated like a refrain in recovery. Had he steered his deputy to the path of recovery, had he nurtured his early steps? Hood had been advised, often, that recovery was for people who want it, not necessarily for those who need it. But he wondered if he had encouraged Young John to want it.

And what was the significance of the two paintings created by Angela thirty years apart? He was contemplating their conversation when Maggie appeared in his office doorway.

"Can I bother you for a minute?"

"Sure."

"I found out Randy Knaebel's father is Dr. Stephen Daniels."

"Me, too," Hood said. "Angela clued me in." He noticed Maggie's expression sour momentarily when he mentioned Angela.

"Does it mean anything—to the case, I mean?"

"I don't know. There's something missing here, something I'm not picking up on. Dr. Daniels was at Randy's trial setting, which makes sense now that I know they're father and son. But Angela heard the doctor whistling a tune in the hallway, and it caused her to paint a picture that matches one she created when she was a kid."

"You lost me," Maggie said.

"Yeah, sorry. Just thinking out loud."

"How's Linda?"

"She's good," Hood said, although he had no idea if that was true. "Why?"

Maggie winced slightly in response to the defensive brusqueness in his tone. "Just asking. I haven't seen her for a while."

"She's fine."

"Good," Maggie said.

"Okay."

Although Maggie understood their conversation was over, she lingered in the doorway. "Francis," she said, "if there's anything you need to talk about—"

"Everything's good."

As she walked away, he wondered who he was trying to convince with his assurance.

Hood's eyes widened when he saw his wife's van parked in the driveway at their home.

He parked haphazardly beside it and rushed to the house. The front door was ajar. He walked briskly toward the kitchen but stopped when her voice hailed him from the living room. "In here," she called.

He backed up two steps and looked into the space where he had clustered the furniture in the center. Linda sat on one of the drop cloths covering a portion of the floor bordering the freshly painted walls.

"It's beautiful."

Hood was momentarily stumped, then realized she was referring to the pristine coat of Pale Bluebell paint.

"Thanks," he said. "Any news?" he asked, abruptly changing the subject.

"All good," she replied as she stood. "The lump's benign. They want to remove it, but it's a routine procedure."

Hood felt relief course through his body, releasing tension so deep he didn't realize he had been amassing it.

Observing his reaction, Linda said, "It's been a tough time."

Hood approached her with open arms and embraced her. He savored the moment, the mutual joy of emerging from a potential ordeal.

"How are you doing?" she whispered in his ear.

He released her, and they separated to arms' length, still holding hands. "I'm okay. I'm not drinking, if that's what you mean." He wanted to be honest and say he was lonely and miserable. He wanted, again, to encourage her and Elizabeth to return home, but had promised himself he wouldn't repeat a subject he knew was painful for her. "I still get cravings, but those times are fewer and farther between. Matthew says the obsession will go away eventually."

"I miss you, Francis. Elizabeth does, too."

He nodded. "Me, too," he said, resisting the temptation to say more.

"This experience has gotten me thinking. I'm more, I don't know, we never know how much time—" She left the sentence unfinished, allowing a momentary pause to float between them.

"Come here," he said, stepping forward in a renewed embrace. He felt her buried against his neck and shoulder. He felt her shudder, followed by an audible sob. "I'm here, Linda, sweetheart. Just know that when you're ready, I'll be here."

Angela was in the kitchen scooping dog food into Prince's bowl when Odessa entered.

"Want me to take him for a walk when he's done eating?" Odessa asked.

"I'll do it. It's a beautiful fall day, and a walk might do me good."

"Something on your mind?"

Although Odessa tried to sound casual, Angela felt the weight of the question. "Is it that obvious?"

"We've known each other a long time. After a while, you pick up on moods, rhythms. I know this is a trying time— with the assaults, the sheriff's questioning."

"Follow me," Angela instructed.

She left the kitchen, trailed by Odessa and Prince, who abandoned the remainder of his meal.

They entered the studio, where Angela explained the timetable and inspiration of the two "Amazing Grace" paintings.

When she finished, Odessa said, "Let me see if I've got this right. You recall Dr. Daniels whistling that tune while he was here, in this house, when you were seven, about a year before the rampage?"

"Yes."

"So that would have been before—"

"Before David was born. Brian would have been a toddler then."

Odessa twisted her mouth into a frown but said nothing.

"I went to see Randy," Angela continued. "He told me his mother took him and left because she thought her husband was cheating on her. Her husband, Randy's father, is Dr. Daniels."

Odessa considered the information. "Do you think—"

"That my mother and Dr. Daniels were having an affair," Angela said, completing the thought. "That's all I've been thinking about."

"Do you remember if your father was home during those

times when the doctor was here?"

"I've been wracking my brain over it. I can't remember."

Odessa was quiet for a long moment before she said, "What are you going to do?"

"I think I need to visit the doctor."

CHAPTER

22

Hood backed his cruiser into a spot in the lot at Doctors Park Medical Plaza. He was about to open the door when he noticed Hutch's pickup truck—with Jacob in the passenger seat—exit the parking area.

Minutes later, Hood was seated in Dr. Daniels' third-floor office, where he was told the doctor would be with him as soon as he finished dictating notes from his last appointment.

As Hood waited, he scanned the room, finally focusing on an anatomical illustration of a human head, including ear canal, nasal cavity, and throat. His inspection of the details—maxillary sinuses, eustachian tubes, and pharynx—ended abruptly when the doctor entered.

The two men greeted each other, and Hood again noted the haunted, vacant look in the doctor's deep-set eyes. Now, at least, he had some explanation—Daniels had been divorced for decades, his ex-wife had died, and his son was estranged.

"So, what's on your mind?" Daniels asked. He sat at his desk.

Hood repositioned one of the visitors' chairs and sat.

"I've been thinking about the assaults on Jacob Grace. Is there any common denominator about these mutilations?"

"As you know, doctor-patient confidentiality—"

"C'mon Stephen," Hood coaxed, intentionally using the doctor's given name. "I'm not asking for anything I don't already know. I'm just trying to find a connection. All these attacks strike me as carefully orchestrated. I hate to use the word superficial, but none of these wounds has been life-threatening. I mean, who cuts somebody's throat but not deeply enough to do any real damage?"

Daniels shrugged. "I don't know what to tell you."

"You said a sharp blade was used on the ear. The EMT at Hutch's thought a limb-lopper of some kind may have been used on Jacob's nose. And I was told his throat was cut by some kind of serrated blade."

"Sounds right."

"But why?" Hood asked. "Why different weapons?"

His question met with silence until Daniels ventured, "Maybe the assailant chose the most efficient tool for the job."

Hood sat upright, attentive. "How so?"

"Sharp blade for the outer ear cartilage, shears to pinch and sever the nose, serrated blade for the more tender skin at the throat."

While the sheriff considered the hypothesis, Daniels glanced at the clock on his desktop. "I need to leave soon," he said.

"Sure. I, uh, I'll—" Hood replied, obviously deep in thought. "I need to think about what you've said."

"Hope it helps."

The men shook hands, and Hood left.

Thoughts whirled and collided in the sheriff's mind as he rode the elevator to the lobby. When the door opened, he stepped out and nearly ran into Angela. Prince intervened, squeezing himself between them, and Hood immediately stepped back.

"Sheriff," she exclaimed. "I didn't expect to see you here."

"I had some questions for Dr. Daniels. And you?"

"The same."

"He told me he was leaving. Is he expecting you?"

"No."

"Can it wait?" Hood asked. "I'd like to get your thoughts on something."

She hesitated. "Why not?"

They crossed the hallway to a coffee bar, where Hood ordered a chai tea requested by Angela and a dark roast coffee for himself. They sat at a small table near a wall of windows overlooking the hallway and front entrance.

"So," Hood said, "what did you want to talk about with the doctor?"

Angela took a straw from her purse, removed the sanitary wrapper, and stuck it through the plastic slit in the lid of her cup. Hood interpreted the gesture as a stalling tactic.

"I think my mom and Dr. Daniels were having an affair back then."

"What makes you think so?"

"I can't be sure, but it would make sense. My parents

had a terrible argument on the night of the rampage. My father was in one of his drunken stupors. If my mother had admitted the affair, that might have been what set him off."

"But why attack her? Why not retaliate against the doctor?"

"Maybe my mother wouldn't tell him who she was having the affair with. Maybe he never knew."

Hood contemplated the explanation.

"Why did *you* want to see Dr. Daniels?" Angela asked.

"I'm trying to learn if the assaults—the wounds, the weapons—have anything in common. I mean, first an ear, then the nose, the throat."

Hood and Angela both watched through the glass as Dr. Daniels exited the elevator, walked briskly along the hallway and out the door.

"He's leaving," Angela said.

In that moment, the revelation—ear, nose, and throat—struck Hood with the force of a gut punch. *Ear, nose, and throat.* Could it be Dr. Daniels' idea of a macabre joke? *Ear, nose and throat*—Jacob's wounds, the doctor's specialty.

"Let's go," Hood said.

"Go where?"

"Wherever he's going,"

They exited as Daniels' white Mercedes moved toward the exit and turned onto Madison Street.

"I'm parked right here," Angela clicked a key fob to unlock her Cadillac SUV and handed the keys to Hood. "You drive."

With Angela in the passenger seat and Prince in the back,

Hood sped onto Madison. He kept the Mercedes in sight and, when it turned westbound onto four-lane Highway 50, he maneuvered between the lanes and closed the distance.

When the Mercedes' turn indicator signaled a right onto Route AA—the vicinity of Angela's farm—she asked, "Where do you think he's headed?"

"No idea."

He and Angela sat silently. Traffic along AA was light, and Hood purposely slowed the SUV to increase the distance between the vehicles. He glanced periodically in the rear-view mirror to check on Prince, who appeared to be enjoying the ride.

In the Cadillac's quiet interior, he heard Angela's audible sigh of relief as the Mercedes passed the driveway to her house and turned north onto Old Cedar Creek Road.

"Hutch's place?" Hood ventured.

"Why there?"

"That's where your father's been living—in Hutch's stable."

Angela shook her head, indicating surprise. "I had no idea."

Hood followed patiently, watching warily, as the Mercedes turned into Hutch's farm and proceeded slowly down the gravel drive to the stable.

He scanned his surroundings for cover and parked behind a copse of pine trees that sheltered the SUV from being seen from the stable.

Hood and Angela quietly exited the vehicle, and they watched from their vantage point as the doctor entered the stable through a partially open, large sliding door. Daniels carried a small implement neither of them recognized.

"Let's go," Hood whispered to Angela.

She nodded, opening the door of the SUV to release Prince, and the trio hurried along the gravel drive.

Hood sidled to the open stable door and peered inside. Angela stood beside him, peeking through a gap where a sliver of weathered wood had become dislodged from the aging planks that formed the walls.

Together, they watched as Daniels, in the dim light of the interior, crept slowly along the center aisle flanked by stalls on either side.

His movements stirred the horses to whinny expectations their visitor might replenish their oats or, preferably, treat them to apple slices or sugar cubes.

The doctor looked inside the cubical that served as Jacob's spartan bedroom, the site of Hood's previous search for the missing nose. When Daniels turned around, Hood noted the doctor's expression revealed both surprise and confusion.

Daniels stood quietly and listened. With the exception of random whinnies and snorts among the horses, the interior was still. After several moments, he began walking the length of the stable. His footfalls on the sawdust floor were soundless as he crossed the center aisle.

The tranquil silence of the scene had lulled Hood, so much so that he shuddered when he saw Jacob Grace—armed with a pitchfork—emerge from an open stall behind the doctor. Hood heard Angela gasp.

Jacob crossed the aisle and poked the pitchfork tines into

Daniels' back. "Turn around," Jacob commanded.

The doctor stiffened, then turned slowly, and faced Jacob.

"What's that?" Jacob demanded, gesturing with his head toward the device the doctor held.

"Bone saw."

Jacob's grin was simultaneously malevolent and amused. "And what were you planning to do with that?"

The doctor didn't answer.

"Well, drop it."

Daniels stooped slightly and dropped the saw.

As he straightened, Jacob pressed the pitchfork tines against the doctor's throat and stepped forward, forcing Daniels to retreat until his back was pinned against the wooden stable enclosure.

"I didn't take the pill," Jacob said, as if he owed some explanation to the physician. "I put two and two together after that last visit to your office. I fell asleep afterward while working on the fence and got my throat cut," he pointed to the bandage circling his neck, "I figured the pills you were giving me were knocking me out."

Daniels said nothing. He pressed himself against the wood, trying to ease the sting of the pitchfork tines poking his throat.

Hood glanced at Angela, who used her upraised hands, palms open, to ask what they should do. Hood mouthed the words "not yet," then turned his attention back to the confrontation within.

"I've been figuring out a lot of things," Jacob said.

"Like what?" Daniels asked.

"It was you who had an affair with my wife," Jacob said. His tone was loud and forceful, but not a shout. "She told me she was having an affair—that night when I went crazy with rage—but not with who. I was all drugged up and boozed up. I beat her, but she wouldn't tell me who. Then the knife was in my hand, and it was just a fit of stabbing and slashing and blood, and I just kept on. I followed her to the front porch, still cutting—then I must have gone to the kitchen and upstairs, but I don't remember—" Jacob stopped, his energy spent from the recollection. He pointed to his bandaged face. "Is that why you did this? Because of her?"

Dr. Daniels looked into Jacob's eyes. "And my son."

"Your son?"

"Not Randy, not my son by marriage," the doctor said. "David, my son by Ruth, your wife. She told me David was my son, not yours." He choked out the words as his sobs began coming in waves "And you—you killed him. You killed him in his crib."

Jacob pulled back the pitchfork in apparent preparation to strike, then hesitated.

In that moment, Hood heard Angela's whispered command, and Prince sprinted past the sheriff into the stable and raced toward Jacob.

Amid the commotion, Jacob turned and pointed the pitchfork at Prince in an effort to fend off the attack.

Daniels swiped at the implement and knocked it to the ground in the instant when the German Shepherd sprang on

Jacob and took him to the ground.

Prince showed his fangs and growled a guttural warning as he straddled Jacob's chest.

Hood and Angela rushed to the scene. The sheriff watched as Daniels looked furtively for a possible escape route before reconsidering and remaining still.

Angela quieted Prince and called him to her side, where the dog remained a menacing presence focused on the two strangers.

Jacob rolled onto his back and looked at her. "Angela?"

Hood noted her nod of acknowledgement was barely perceptible.

"I don't know—" Jacob stammered. "There's so much—I just—"

She turned to Hood, who interpreted her expression of unease. He moved to her and whispered, "Almost done." He called the department for backup and ordered Jacob and Daniels to stand on opposite sides of the entrance to an empty stall. When they were in position, Hood cuffed one of Jacob's wrists, fed the other cuff through a floor-to-ceiling stud of the door jamb and secured Daniels' wrist to the remaining cuff. Then he closed the door, securing and separating the two men.

"Clever," Angela observed.

"Learned that the hard way." He smiled at the recollection of being handcuffed to Young John through a refrigerator door handle. "Why don't you go ahead and take off?"

"You sure?"

"I'm sure."

"Thanks," Angela said.

"Thank you." Hood stooped and patted Prince's flank. "You, too. You did good, boy."

Hood watched as they retreated along the stable's long aisle and disappeared beyond the door.

CHAPTER

23

Hood leaned against the front fender of his cruiser, which was parked on the macadam road that weaved a serpentine path through the cemetery.

The grassy expanse had browned in places, yielding to dormancy in anticipation of winter. Headstones, from simple markers to customized monuments, protruded from the ground in an orderly alignment.

From his vantage point, he watched the distant figures of Angela and Prince, who sat beside where Angela stood with her back to Hood. She faced a wide granite stone, seemingly unaware of the sheriff's presence.

Hood waited. He waited while dusk gathered, waited until Angela finally turned and, with Prince matching her stride, approached.

She wore dark slacks with a tan turtleneck and suede jacket. A veil, rather than a mask, hid the lower portion of her face. If she was surprised to see him, neither her eyes nor her movements betrayed it.

"Sorry," he said. "I didn't mean to intrude. Odessa told me you'd be out here. I've got—"

"You're not intruding," Angela said. "I'm glad you're here. It's their anniversary—of their deaths, I mean."

"I know." Hood said. "I remembered."

Angela nodded. "What's next?"

"My work, the investigation, is done. This is where everything gets turned over to the courts."

"What do you think will happen?"

Hood shrugged. "I no longer predict what the courts will do. I used to think the system determined truth and assessed reasonable punishment, but I know now that's rarely the case. The justice system is messy, and the verdicts sometimes are far from fair."

"You think that will happen with Dr. Daniels?"

"We'll see," Hood answered "He's been charged with three counts of aggravated assault. They're felonies, and they were premeditated—I mean, he had 30 years to plan them— but how much of that can be proved? There were no witnesses, no body parts recovered, and no weapons except the bone saw he brought to the stable. Who knows what a jury will decide?"

"What about my father?"

"What about him?" Hood repeated. "He was the victim until he confronted the doctor in the stable, but you prevented him from any retaliation."

"Prince did," she corrected.

"Okay," Hood said, "but Prince was responding to your

command. I know you may not want to think so, but you spared your father from a lot of heartache and, probably, a lot more prison time."

They faced each other in silence for a long, awkward moment before Hood said, "Well, I guess that's it then."

"Maybe I'll see you around the courthouse," Angela said. "Randy's attorney is working out a plea bargain. He's decided to plead guilty to the robberies."

Hood nodded.

"I think I'm going to miss you dropping by without an appointment," Angela said.

Hood smiled. "Maybe I'll stop by just to annoy Odessa."

Her eyes suggested a smile. "I've got an exhibition coming up in St. Louis in the spring. Would you and your family like to come—as my guests?"

"I'll ask."

"I'll call you with the specifics."

"Thanks," Hood said. As Angela and Prince walked to her SUV, he added, "for everything."

Hood felt a measure of queasiness as he waited for Linda. The idea of feeling anxious to see a woman he had known intimately for decades seemed nonsensical but he couldn't deny what he was experiencing.

She toted a cloth bag when Hood opened the front door to her. In the hallway, they hugged and kissed in a brief, casual greeting that was customary before their separation.

"What have you got there?" Hood asked, gesturing toward the bag.

"Some fabric swatches." I was thinking about making curtains for our newly painted living room. Pinch pleats are tricky, but I've done it before."

Hood felt encouraged, both by her desire to make curtains and her reference to *our* living room, but he said nothing.

"I'd like your opinion if you have time."

"Sure."

"How's everything?" she asked, as they walked into the living room.

"Good. It's good. I told you we arrested Dr. Daniels for the assaults on Jacob Grace."

"Yes. And I read the news articles. I'm glad that's over."

"Why?"

"It seemed to be taking a toll on you," Linda replied. "Besides, if I'm being totally honest, I was a little jealous of Angela."

"She invited us—all of us, you, me, and Elizabeth—to a show she has coming up in St. Louis."

"When?"

"In the spring. I don't know the dates yet."

"But you'd like to go?"

"I'd like all of us to go." He paused. "You don't need to worry about Angela. I mean, I admit I was curious about her. She's a human puzzle, but I realize now my attempt to figure her out was really an attempt to understand myself—my own thoughts, feelings, emotions, motivations, beliefs—everything."

"Relationships?"

"I haven't been able to stop wondering where our relationship is going, but I know now all I can do is try to be better and trust things will work out."

"I've got some work to do in that area as well." She stooped over the bag and rummaged among the fabric swatches, which Hood interpreted as a sign to change the subject.

"I've got a little of everything," she added, "from some sedate, complimentary solid colors to some bold plaids and prints."

When she stood, holding a variety of samples, Hood approached and embraced her. "I'm so sorry," he whispered. When she didn't pull away or abbreviate the embrace, he added, "I love you so much."

Linda lingered in his arms. "I've missed you," she said. "I've been missing you for a long time. Even before I left, you just gradually disappeared, and I couldn't be here and watch it anymore. Once I realized I couldn't change it, I knew I had to leave. It's not that I stopped loving you; I just couldn't stay with the alcoholic you'd become."

"I understand that now."

"It was the hardest thing I've ever done."

Hood squeezed her, gently, then released his grasp. They stood close to each other, face to face.

"You've changed, Francis," Linda said. "You're becoming a different person."

"I am," he agreed. "When the people in recovery talked about finding a higher power, I think I expected some bright light and thunderclap of revelation—even some feeling of salvation—but that hasn't happened. I realize now that recovery is a gradual process of self-discovery—of transformation—of getting comfortable with who I am. Little by little, I'm developing a faith that works in everyday life. I'm enjoying some peace and serenity, and I'm okay with that."

"I like this new Francis."

"Me too."

Silence ensued.

Finally, Linda looked at the samples she held in each hand. She walked to the window and held one where they could evaluate how it worked with blue walls, white window frame and natural light.

"What do you think?" she asked.

Hood thought everything was going to be okay.

THE END

Acknowledgements

"Will you tell us a story, Daddy?"

Today, my daughters are adults, but their childhood interest in hearing stories is among my fondest memories. My wife is an avid reader, and our household remains a place where books abound and where reading and creating stories are valued. I am eternally grateful for the love and support from my wife Kristie, daughters Heather and Jane, and my extended family.

Stories combine imagination and expertise, and often require knowledge I do not possess. My thanks to friends in the professional community who graciously answered my questions relating to medical, mental health, law enforcement and judicial issues. They include Michael Van Gundy, MS, licensed professional counselor; former Cole County Sheriff Greg White; Cole County Presiding Circuit Judge Patricia Joyce; and Dr. Douglas Howland, DO. Any factual or procedural errors are mine.

I also am indebted to people who read early drafts of my work and offered suggestions. In addition to my wife, they include Phil Baker, Madeleine Leroux, and Rebecca Martin.

In addition, I appreciate the keen insights and recommendations of G.B. Crump, R.M. Kinder, and James H. Taylor, my editors at Cave Hollow Press.

Finally, thanks to my "other" family for sharing their experience and encouragement.

About the Author

Richard F. McGonegal and his wife Kristie live in Jefferson City, MO, where their two adult daughters Heather and Jane also reside. He retired in 2017 after a 41-year journalism career at the *Jefferson City News Tribune*. Twenty-four of his short stories have been published in magazines, including *Alfred Hitchcock's Mystery Magazine*. *Sense of Grace* is his first published novel.

CPSIA information can be obtained
at www.ICGtesting.com
Printed in the USA
LVHW010611190720
661015LV00002B/182

9 781734 267808